a Line of Duty novel

STAKING
His Claim

a *Line of Duty* novel

STAKING His Claim

#1 *NEW YORK TIMES* BESTSELLING AUTHOR
TESSA BAILEY

Entangled Publishing, LLC
644 Shrewsbury Commons Ave
STE 181
Shrewsbury, PA 17361
rights@entangledpublishing.com

Brazen is an imprint of Entangled Publishing, LLC.

Edited by Heather Howland
Cover design by LJ Anderson/Mayhem Cover Creations
Cover photography by anatoliycherkas/Depositphotos

Manufactured in the United States of America

First Edition February 2014

ENTANGLED
BRAZEN

Chapter One

The studio audience inside Lucy Mason's head gave a collective, sympathetic *awww*.

Ditched again.

"This was supposed to be *our* week, Sasha." Lucy picked up her iced coffee and plunked it back down, never taking her gaze off her best friend. "Ill-advised exploits, questionable fashion choices. Educational museum trips." She mumbled that last part, since it hadn't exactly been part of their monthlong discussion. "I can't believe you're blowing me off for a dude."

Sasha winced. "I know. I know. It's just…*Carter*."

"Carter." Lucy's brow wrinkled. "Is this the same Carter who made a pass at your mom when she came to visit?"

"That was a misunderstanding."

"I'll just bet." She moved her drink in jerky circles on the table, letting the tinkling ice cool it even further, hoping a sip would cool the fire in her throat, brought on by the need to shout. Minutes before she and her roommate were set to depart Syracuse University, where they'd both, at *long* last, completed their respective master's programs, and her plans were being crushed by a guy who'd once pissed himself on their couch after too much tequila. Unacceptable. As if this violation of the "chicks before dicks manifesto" weren't bad enough, her brother, Brent, who'd been their designated ride to New York City, had bailed at the last minute.

God, I'm sorry, Luce. Something came up with Hayden's family. She's presenting her father with some fancy-ass award and if I don't go, she'll castrate me.

Her brother wasn't one to hold back. Even if it meant talking to his sister about his balls. Going to live with him in their childhood house in Queens at the age of twenty-five was going to be a real scream. Until she became gainfully employed and found her own place, that is. Thanks to her growing list of potential employers alphabetically arranged in an Excel spreadsheet, it wouldn't be long. In the meantime, she'd have to set some ground rules, like no testicular talk. Or making out with his fiancée anywhere her eyeballs might encounter it.

In his place today, her brother had sent his friend Matt Donovan. Another cop. One she'd never met, but based on Brent's suggestion to bring oodles of reading material for the drive, she gathered Matt was not a sparkling conversationalist. It hadn't bothered her much, knowing she'd have Sasha to chat with in the backseat, but now that option was no longer on the table. Truth be told, she felt a little slighted.

Okay, a lot slighted. Her brother and best friend making for greener pastures within twenty-four hours of each other didn't do fabulous things for her ego. They hadn't meant it that way, she rationalized. They loved her. Still, it was two more instances she could add to her list of times she'd come in second place. Lucy Mason, salutatorian. First runner-up at the debate team finals as an undergrad. Hell, just this week she'd been named second in her class, among the other language majors. While these were certainly accomplishments, sometimes it felt like no matter how hard she tried, someone always beat her by an inch. Sasha and Brent ditching her for their respective lovers was no different.

Pity party of one, your table is ready.

Trying to dispel the useless feeling, she took a long pull on her iced coffee. Sasha had a healthy glow to her deep-brown skin, excitement shining in her eyes that hadn't been there this morning. Just because *she* hadn't had sex since *Lost* was on the air didn't give her the right to be a begrudger. "So what are your plans instead? You better be doing something amazing. Seriously, I want goose bumps."

Sasha did a little dance in her seat, accompanied by a squeal. "We're borrowing his cousin's house at Cayuga Lake. Just me, Carter, and a handful of naughty DVDs."

Lucy perked up. "What? Like porn?"

"No. Like *Cruel Intentions* and *Wild Things*. Movies where girls make out so as to guarantee a good evening for yours truly." Sasha tilted her head. "By the way, you have never looked as enthusiastic in your *life* as you just did when porn entered the equation."

"Lower your voice," Lucy whispered.

"Porn-o-graph-y!" Sasha belted out, opera-style, drawing every eye in the coffeehouse.

Lucy shook her head. "I'm so not going to miss you."

"Liar. You will *pine* for me."

"If you drown in Cayuga Lake, I will clear out your sex toy stash as promised, but that's all I can guarantee you. Not a single line of poetry will be penned in your honor."

"At lease I'll die happy." Sasha rose and came to join Lucy on the bench, where she crushed her in a tight hug. "Hey, I'm really sorry. You know that, right?"

"Yeah," Lucy murmured into her friend's hair. "Now go on. Get."

Sasha pulled back to study her. "Listen, if I die in an unfortunate water skiing accident or too many orgasms—"

"Or both."

"Or both." Sasha nodded. "Don't dump my stash. I hereby bequeath all manner of pleasure machines to you, my pasty, studious little friend."

Lucy feigned surprised pleasure. "Me? I-I don't know what to say."

"Say you'll put New York on its knees this week." Her friend's expression suddenly turned serious. "Don't use my bailing as an excuse to hole up with a stack of books. You've earned some fun, graduate. Have at it."

Lucy stared after Sasha thoughtfully as she exited the coffee shop. Her friend knew her too well. Initially, when Sasha canceled on her, there had been a tiny little punch of relief in her chest that she was off the hook. That she wouldn't have to put herself out there as planned, but could continue her two-year streak of hiding from the unknown. Safe in her self-imposed introversion. She hadn't always been this way. No, no. Her first four years in college had been spent exploring the Mason daredevil gene she'd inherited. Right up until she'd organized an on-campus bonfire in protest of censorship in their textbooks, landing her in jail overnight. Hello wake-up call. Needless to say, her brother had lost his shit *and* been forced to re-mortgage his house to bail her out. Not to mention covering the fines she'd incurred.

Since her night in the big house, she'd spent her days and nights busting her ass to make her family proud, instead of inspiring ceaseless rounds of head-shaking every time her name came up. Making sure Brent knew she didn't take for granted the tuition he worked two jobs to provide. In the very near future, she would have a job that would finally ease the pressure from his shoulders. She could finally pitch in to support her parents and her other older brother's family while he fought overseas. Her family would take pride in her, instead of taking cover every time she entered the room.

That staunch dedication to success hadn't left room for much more, and she'd allowed her social life to dwindle until Sasha's recaps of Saturday nights were her main source of entertainment. As soon as she had a steady income and a place to call her own, she'd been planning to remedy that oversight. Then again, maybe Sasha had a valid point. What better place to kick off her new lecture- and homework-free life than a week in New York City?

The bell tinkled over the coffee shop door, drawing Lucy's attention. Had Sasha changed her mind? Or maybe she'd forgotten someth—

Lucy's thoughts drained, as if her brain had turned into a colander. Every muscle in her body coiled tightly as a man stepped right out of every woman's fantasy and somehow materialized in the coffee shop. Before anything else registered, she noticed the way he walked. He moved like he was walking toward a lover. A lover he planned on thoroughly roughing up before making her scream obscenities into a pillow. The sensual, detached movement of his hips was a complete contradiction to his eyes and jaw, however. They were set firmly, making him look ruthless. Unmovable.

Dark hair, dark expression, dark clothing. He was just… several shades of dark. Except for his eyes, she amended as he coolly scanned the shop. His eyes were light gray. In the midst of all that darkness, they stood out like silvery marcasite.

She couldn't stop her gaze from tracking downward, over broad shoulders, a wide chest, and a heavy leather belt that rode low on his waist. As if a good stretch would reveal his happy trail and that cut vee leading into his jeans. Speaking of jeans, good Lord, the man's ass was a bona fide work of art. As he strode toward the nearby counter to place his order, his work boots not making a single sound, those tight buns set off a choir of rejoicing angels in her head.

Then he opened his mouth to address the barista and the angels' mouths snapped shut.

"Can you tell me where 39 Juniper Street is located?"

Huh? Lucy's spine went rigid. That was *her* address. Perhaps he was looking for someone else in her building? She and Sasha shared a two-bedroom in an off-campus dwelling, in which there were at least twenty other apartments. That had to be it. This work of male perfection could not be the boring, stuffy ex-military sniper her brother had sent to squire her down to the city. Brent's description could not have painted a different picture. No, this guy had to be looking for someone else.

The barista behind the counter looked like she'd just gone for a swim in a lake full of stupid. "What?" She cleared her throat and smiled. "I mean...what?"

Buns of Glory sighed. "Thirty-nine Juniper. My GPS says it's nearby, so I thought I'd walk the rest of the way. Can you point me in the right direction?"

Another barista joined her. "What?"

Now Lucy sighed on his behalf. Communication must be difficult when your ass whittled the opposite sex's vocabulary down to one word.

"Never mind, I think I can track it down." He gave a faint smile and Lucy swore she could hear panties hit the floor. "I'll take a medium coffee to go. Black."

Not the sugar-and-cream type. No surprises there.

Barista Number One appeared to finally regain her senses. "Are you visiting someone at the college? I haven't seen you here before."

He handed her a crisp bill. "No, I live in Manhattan. I'm just here to pick up a girl."

Oh shit. He is *Matt Donovan.* That was Lucy's first thought. Her second? If her brother had condoned her spending hours in a confined space with this gorgeous man, he had quite a lot to learn about her.

"So...are you picking up just any ol' girl or a specific one?"

Oh, for the love of double Spanx.

"Specific."

"Lucky girl." Barista Number Two with the gem! "She must be pretty special to drive all this way."

Matt took the paper coffee cup she offered. "Actually, from what I hear, she's kind of a nuisance."

Inside Lucy's head, the studio audience broke into a barrage of *oh hell no*'s. She sat up so straight in her booth, she would have feared spinal damage if she could manage to think past her annoyance. A nuisance? On top of her double-ditching that day, the word was like water being poured over hot sauna rocks. They caused her anger to sizzle and snap dangerously. Somewhere underneath all that, a stab of hurt existed, but she didn't want to acknowledge that just yet.

He picked that moment to turn and lock eyes with her across the ten feet separating them. She had the satisfaction of watching his coffee cup pause halfway to his mouth before continuing its journey toward sculpted, masculine lips. Long-denied heat trickled through her, cutting right through her bout of self-pity. Desire. It had been a long time since she'd felt it. Perhaps that was why it tumbled through her midsection now after having been raveled up for years. As if he'd projected the image into her head, she saw those distracting lips feasting on her neck. A neck that had surely turned candy-apple red thanks to the direction of her thoughts.

Feeling this insistent attraction to her brother's best friend was inconvenient at best. Nor could she act on it. Based on what she'd been told about him, he was the honorable type. The voice of reason in their dude foursome. He would never make a move on "Brent's little sister." Especially when said little sister had been painted as nothing more than an irritating pest.

Unless, of course, he didn't know *who* he was putting the moves on.

Matt still watched her closely, but his expression showed no signs of recognition. Apparently Brent hadn't passed on a formal dossier complete with recent photos, because Matt was looking her over in a very *on*-limits kind of way. And boy oh boy, she liked it. Her nerve endings were tingling, nipples pebbling underneath her tank top in a way that had nothing to do with the air-conditioning. When his attention shifted to her bare legs visible beneath her cutoff shorts, warmth settled between her thighs. Was it her imagination or had he just growled at her?

Lying about her identity would be wrong. So very wrong. She couldn't do it. Could she? Her ethics professor would shit a brick. Not to mention, something told her this man wouldn't take kindly to being duped. Her only alternative was to stand up right now and introduce herself as Lucy Mason before it was too late. It would guarantee she arrived safely in Queens, untouched. Hot and bothered with no weapon to combat it, save the five-fingered one attached to her wrist. No closer to shedding the boredom wrought by the last two years.

It sounded horrible, but she was woman enough to admit that, on top of wanting this insanely hot man, her ego needed a little boost. She'd been dateless for too long, she'd been ditched by everyone, and now she'd been labeled a nuisance. Maybe just this once, she could get hers and say to hell with the consequences, the way she used to. The dormant daredevil inside her stretched and looked around sleepily.

Lucy pushed back her chair and stood. Pasting what she hoped was a flirtatious smile on her face, she walked toward Matt and extended her hand. "I couldn't help but overhear that you're looking for 39 Juniper."

He grunted into his coffee. Not exactly the reaction she'd been looking for. No matter, she'd just have to try again. After all, she hadn't gotten to be second place in every competition under the sun without learning a few tricks along the way. Garnering her courage, she ran a hand through her curls and cocked one hip. His teeth sank into his lower lip. There. Now she had his attention. "I'm Sasha, Lucy Mason's roommate. Looks like you're here to give me a ride."

Chapter Two

Hop on, baby. I'll give you a fucking ride.

The thought blew swift and furious through Matt's consciousness before he banished it, locking it safely behind a steel-reinforced door. This girl, the one who stood in front of him looking like a virgin sacrifice sent to tempt his sanity, wouldn't last five minutes with him before she ran off screaming. He *knew* that, and yet he couldn't look away.

Her deliciously unpainted mouth moved and words came out, but it took his brain an extra second to catch on. One hell of a feat, since he prided himself on staying razor sharp at all times. His training had drilled the importance of being consistently alert into his head. His profession demanded it. Yet in under a minute, this girl had managed to test that will, effectively cutting off all blood flow to his brain and sending it straight to his groin.

Fuck, she'd made him hard. In public, no less. Before uttering a single word.

On some level, he resented that.

She *had* spoken, however, and was now looking at him

awaiting a response. What had she said? *Sasha. Wants a ride. Focus, Donovan. You're acting like one of your friends, drooling over some girl, when you know that shit isn't for you.* Will never, *ever*, be for you.

Matt took a sip of his coffee to buy himself some time. Now he remembered why the name Sasha rang a bell. Lucy Mason's roommate. The roommate he'd agreed to share a vehicle with for the next couple hours on the drive back to New York City. Jesus. At least he'd have Brent's pesky sister riding shotgun, preventing him from doing something patently unwise. Like pulling over at the first opportunity and divesting this girl of her frayed jean shorts in his backseat.

Get a handle on it. Now. Before you can't.

Reluctantly, he dragged his gaze away from the embodiment of temptation before him and skimmed a glance over the coffee shop, looking for an entirely different girl. One resembling a linebacker. With a brother the size of a small mountain, Lucy couldn't be too far behind. No luck. As far as he could tell, there wasn't a single fart joke–telling Brent look-alike among this crowd. Although to be fair, he didn't have a clue *what* Lucy looked like, nor had he had time to find out. Driving to Syracuse had been a last-minute favor to his friend, one he'd grudgingly accepted under threat of being forced to endure an afternoon of wedding plan details. He hadn't been able to get behind the wheel fast enough.

"She's not coming," said the temptation, her voice low and smoky. "Lucy, that is."

"Excuse me?"

"Lucy blew us off for her newest boyfriend and his lake house. It's just you and me." She shoved her hands into her pockets, anchoring them lower on her hips. God*damn*.

Matt welcomed the spark of irritation over this new development, hoping it would distract him from the succulence of her navel. No dice. Did she know what she was doing? She had to. It was impossible for a female to radiate that kind of come-and-get-it sexuality without realizing and utilizing it to her advantage. Any amount of time spent alone with her would be a mistake. Lucy's bailing on Brent, and in turn *him*, was an annoyance in itself. Toss in five foot three inches of gorgeous, fresh-faced girl and he was entering dangerous territory.

Miles away from his usual type, she shouldn't be affecting him this way. When he occasionally let himself explore the need he kept shoved down deep inside him, he went for curvier women. Women with some meat on their bones who could withstand what he dished out. The girl peeking up at him under strawberry-blond curls was what men commonly referred to as a "spinner." Petite, passionate, and pliable… one you could switch into a different sexual position without removing yourself from her heat.

While these thoughts were doing nothing to alleviate the growing problem in his jeans, they reminded him why he couldn't have her. He'd had enough women make passes at him in his life that he knew an invitation when he saw it. If he chose to interpret the flirtatious curve of her mouth, the swaying of her hips as an offer, his particular form of accepting that offer would send her packing. Right now, she looked at him and saw a decent-looking man, a departure from the younger, hoodie-sporting guys she met on campus. She didn't see what lurked beneath. The side of him that would come out once he got her naked. Her playful demeanor would turn to shock in a heartbeat. He'd scare the hell out of her.

"That is, if you don't mind me bumming a ride." Her smile had started to slip in his extended silence. "You wouldn't leave a girl stranded, would you?"

Oh yes, she knew exactly what she was doing. Appealing to his protectiveness, his former military, present law enforcement side. Apparently Lucy had passed on basic information about him before blowing everyone the hell off. When he saw a flash of irritation cross her features when he didn't answer right away, lust twisted in his midsection. She had fire, this one. Still, he needed to make damn sure he kept his distance. She was not for him. Even if his impulses were demanding he throw her over his shoulder and find the nearest, darkest corner to introduce his tongue to her stomach, lower.

Distance. Boundaries. He cleared his throat. "How fast can you get your things? I need to get back to the city."

She arched an eyebrow. "Our apartment is across the street. Meet you outside in ten?"

"Fine. Get moving."

He actually saw her teeth sink into her tongue. To keep from shouting? Why did that make him feel like laughing? Instead, she turned on a sandaled heel and marched out of the coffeehouse, giving him an uninterrupted view of her ass swishing in those brief jean shorts. Fuck. Keeping his hands off her for the next four hours was going to be a challenge. Hopefully his abrupt attitude had bought him the silent treatment, rather than a long car ride full of watching those lips move. Imagining them on his flesh. Imagining them parting on a surprised whimper when he brought his hand down hard on her backside.

Think different thoughts. Now. In an attempt to distract himself, he slipped his cell phone out of his jeans and called Brent, just to make sure the giant idiot knew how thoroughly he and his sister had wasted his time this afternoon. It went straight to voice mail. He checked his watch and saw it was already late afternoon. The function Brent was attending to honor Hayden's father would just be getting under way. Guess the ass-chewing would have to wait until tomorrow.

Matt pinched the bridge of his nose and sighed. He could add today's events to the growing list of reasons he kept mostly to himself. His best friends, Brent and Daniel, were the only ones he'd let get remotely close and they were still kept firmly outside the wrought iron perimeter he'd built around his life three years ago. When his world had imploded.

To be fair, Brent and Daniel hadn't really consulted him in the matter of their presence in his life, just barging in and making themselves at home. He made regular attempts to push them to a safer distance, but they always fought their way back. Involving him. Doing him favors without his knowledge or consent. He wished like hell they wouldn't. Those unsolicited actions obligated him to do things like *this*. Driving four hours to pick up Brent's little sister only to find out she'd lived up to her sterling reputation by ditching the entire trip and leaving him shit out of luck, getting ready to endure an ungodly test of his will.

Sasha. That exotic name didn't fit her at all. She looked like a Stacy. Or a Skipper. Something bouncy to account for those curls that made his hands itch to pull them. Hold her steady while he worked himself in from behind.

Matt dragged a hand down his face. This was going to be the longest four hours of his life. Considering he'd spent a huge chunk of his twenties fighting overseas, spending days at a time monitoring targets from his sniper's perch without moving a muscle, that was truly saying something. Through the window of the coffee shop, he watched Sasha lug a suitcase twice her size across a manicured lawn and plunk herself down on top of it, arms crossed, chin raised.

Five minutes early.

This time, he couldn't help the quiet laugh that escaped him.

• • •

All right, this seduction was *definitely* not going according to plan.

Lucy slid a glance across the console of Matt's sleek black sedan, watching him under the cover of her eyelashes. He hadn't looked at her once since loading her suitcase into the trunk, instead keeping his gray eyes glued to the road, jaw tight with obvious frustration that he'd been saddled with some unknown party for the afternoon. As soon as she'd introduced herself as Sasha, he'd lost his expression of blatant interest, shutting down as if on cue. Surely off-limits little sister didn't encompass little sister's roommate? Based on his closed-off demeanor, it clearly did.

Problem with that? In addition to being attracted to him in a sweaty, breathless way that made her crave an ice bath, he now presented a challenge. That part of her that loved being tested and coming out on top was now stretching and lacing up its sneakers. Even with his unfriendly vibe, maybe even *because* of it, she wanted this man. For the last six years, she'd watched her friends take home men from parties for much lesser reasons. She'd admitted just how *much* she wanted him to herself during her mad dash through her empty apartment, unpacking her razor to shave her legs and bikini line in just under two minutes, before slathering on lotion and breaking for the sidewalk. It would have been a cold day in hell before she took longer than the allotted time. Had he commented on her punctuality? No, he hadn't. Had he even peeked at her newly smooth gams? No, he hadn't.

Phase two it is.

Her game was a little dusty, since she hadn't used it in a couple years. Apart from a short-term boyfriend when she'd studied abroad in France, she'd never had a steady man in her life. Just the odd date and obligatory one-night stands that came with the college experience. Matt would require a little extra oomph. She could practically feel the *do not touch* warning radiating from his side of the car. Why did that turn her on even more?

Lucy sat a little straighter in her seat, casually glancing down at her body. She wasn't half-bad, right? At least, she used to think so. Her boobs had been hidden underneath a Syracuse sweatshirt for so long, they might have shrunk a little from disuse. Her legs might be a whiter shade of pale, but summer had only just started. No one had a tan yet, right? She slumped back down in her seat. Obviously her body wouldn't be her most useful tool on this mission to get laid by this sexy beast of a cop. She'd just have to dazzle him with her wits.

"So do you make it up to Syracuse often?"

Fail.

Matt shot her a look that said *is she serious*?

"No, I don't. I came to retrieve Lucy." He pushed a hand through his black hair. "I'm not big on sightseeing. Or last-minute plan changes."

"You know, I kind of sensed that." Impatient with herself, she crossed her legs. Wait, had he looked that time? "I don't know what you've heard about Lucy, but she's actually kind of awesome. Don't judge her too harshly. Hot guy with a lake house. You can't pass that up."

"I assure you, I could."

She gasped. "He makes a joke? Pull over, I'm feeling dizzy."

"Maybe it's the smell of that vanilla lotion. How much did you put on exactly?"

That brought her up short. Not only had he noticed her efforts, he'd spent the last half hour being vexed by them. She couldn't get a read on this guy, couldn't get a hint of what he was thinking by looking at his stoic face. With a single finger, she punched and held the button to crack the passenger-side window. "Better?"

A grunt served as his reply. After a minute, though, he

surprised her by breaking the uncomfortable silence. "Major?"

"Sorry?"

His hands flexed on the steering wheel. "You just completed grad school, right? What was your major?"

Shit. She hadn't anticipated the questions. Did he know what Lucy had majored in? Probably not, since he had no clue what she looked like. Of course, the only details Brent would pass on would be her shortcomings. She owed him a nice, sisterly punch in the gut when she got home. For now, it was best to stick with a close version of the truth, so she didn't lose track of fabricated stories. An uneasy feeling settled in her belly. This game wasn't quite as fun as she'd anticipated. "Double major. French language and art history."

He studied her for a moment, appearing to reevaluate her, before returning his attention to the road. No flicker of recognition, though, only surprise. "Do you have plans?"

She nodded. "I have offers from several smaller museums. A few in New York. One in Paris. The Louvre, actually." It felt like a jinx to finally say it out loud. As if voicing the offer of a lifetime, working as a research assistant in the world-famous museum, might make it disappear in a cloud of sparkly dust. She wasn't necessarily thinking about taking the job, since she'd already been away from home for so long. But every once in a while, she'd open the e-mail containing the offer and reread it out loud. In a French accent. "I spent two years studying in Paris and I've always wanted to go back. But I'm taking a week to decide."

"One week?" Another measured glance in her direction. "That's a pretty quick turnaround."

Lucy shrugged. "I've got some business to take care of." Realizing the conversation was turning too personal, not a good idea when she was pretending to be Sasha, she ended that line of questioning by reaching into her purse and pulling out the week's itinerary. If she had to face the city solo, she might have some adjustments to make.

A beat passed. "What's that?"

"My plans for the week. Or *former* plans, I should say. I doubt I can bike tandem through Central Park by myself."

"Lucy left you in the lurch."

"Hot guy. Lake house. *Cruel Intentions* on DVD."

Matt snorted. "What else is on your list, Sasha?"

Something in her chest pinched when he used her roommate's name, but she determinedly cast it aside. "Do you really want to know?"

He frowned at the windshield. "That bad, huh?"

She held the list, pretending to read it. "Crash a wedding at the Waldorf. Rappel down the side of a forty-story building. Break a billionaire's heart."

When he sent her a dark look, she merely winked at him to assure him she'd been joking.

"Very funny."

"About time you noticed."

"Oh, I noticed." His gaze raked her thighs, moved up her belly and over her breasts. The air-conditioning blasting through the interior of the car became totally inadequate as Lucy's body heated like a furnace. "Believe me, I noticed."

Her breath escaped her in a shaky puff. "Yeah? Are you planning on doing anything about it or ignoring me until we reach New York?"

"Ignoring you isn't exactly an option." He sounded almost angry. "Not when you're sitting that close, smelling that damn good, with your thighs falling open to fuck with my head every other mile."

Oh my God. Who the hell was this guy? In the wake of his words, her body began to hum like an electric generator. "Y-you only answered half my question."

His jaw flexed. "I'm dropping you off in New York the same way I picked you up."

"Bored?"

He shook his head. "Clean."

Lucy reeled a little under the impact of his unexpected answer. That single word told her so much about him while at the same time, spawning a hundred more questions. He thought touching her would…tarnish her? It didn't fit in with the arrogance he wore on the surface. She opened her mouth to ask him to clarify what he'd meant, then decided against it. The set of his mouth told her she'd be wasting her time. Delving any deeper would just shut him down completely.

She took a breath and glanced back down at her itinerary. "There's only one important activity on the list. The rest is just funny business."

"Funny business."

Lucy nodded. "Correct. Thursday, however, is important. It's the sixtieth anniversary of my grandfather proposing to my grandmother."

"You're celebrating with them?"

"Actually, Matt, they're dead." She shook her head. "Way to bring up a painful subject."

He shot her a look, smirking when he saw she was kidding.

She let her head fall back on the headrest. "He popped the question on a bench in Central Park. I'm going to be there for the exact minute it happened." She shrugged. "Kind of like a tribute."

"You won't be alone for that, at least. Someone will probably be asleep on it."

She covered her eyes. "Please, stop. Your optimism is blinding me."

Without missing a beat, he handed her his sunglasses. Lucy put them on.

Before she could ask him how he saw through such dark lenses, something under the hood of the car snapped, screeched and fell into a thumping pattern.

"Serpentine belt," Lucy said automatically as Matt cursed, pulling the car onto the shoulder.

"What was that?"

"Nothing." If Matt had spent any amount of time with Brent, he knew about the Mason family obsession with cars. Diagnosing his engine trouble would definitely tip her hand. "I said…I don't like how that felt." He shot her a suspicious look, but ultimately climbed out of the car. She debated a moment, then joined him under the hood he'd propped open. Seeing the frayed belt, she let herself enjoy a little surge of pride at being correct. "Uh-oh. That looks bad."

He was already dialing his phone and didn't answer. When what Lucy assumed to be roadside assistance answered, he rattled off their location perfectly and described in exact detail the engine's condition. His words were clipped and precise, telling her how close attention he paid, even when he appeared to be lost in his own world. She needed to remember that.

"How much is it going to cost to tow it back to New York?" Matt asked into the phone, before wincing at the answer. "How about the closest garage? Fine."

He hung up.

"That sounded promising. Tow back to New York too expensive?"

Matt cast a look down the busy highway. "It literally would have been highway robbery,"

A laugh bubbled from her throat. "At least you've maintained your relentless sense of humor." She stepped back as he closed the hood. "So, what now, Chuckles?"

His throat worked as he grazed her with another head-to-toe perusal. In that moment, she got the odd impression that she made him nervous, but that couldn't be right.

"Good question," he finally answered, with all the enthusiasm of an undertaker.

Chapter Three

He was actually checking into a roadside motel with the rosy-cheeked girl next door. If she knew, if she had even an *inkling* of the thoughts bombarding his mind, she would have taken her chances hitchhiking the rest of the way to New York City.

They'd ridden in the tow truck to the nearest garage, whose mechanic had informed him they could have a serpentine belt ordered for his car by morning. Which meant they were stuck overnight, still three hours from home, in a convenient motel adjacent to the garage.

Convenient. Right.

While they waited for the slow-moving motel clerk to wake up his ancient computer, he decided it would be safer to book her a separate room. He didn't trust himself having her within reaching distance. Throw in a convenient bed and time to kill…he'd be screwed in more ways than one.

Right on cue, the clerk lifted his head. "One room?"

"Yes," Sasha chirped.

"Two," he answered at the same time.

Doing his best to ignore the way her tempting lips pursed

in disapproval, he handed the clerk his credit card. When he saw the man eyeing Sasha with not-so-subtle interest, he nearly snatched it back. He didn't like the look on the clerk's face. In fact, it kind of bothered the shit out of him, especially since he'd brought it on by claiming they required separate rooms. So much for retaining his sanity.

"On second thought, just one room," he said, holding on to the card until the clerk met his eyes. Hopefully, a room with two double beds and a decent enough cable hookup would keep him distracted. Matt almost laughed out loud at that. A teeming swarm of locusts couldn't distract him from her. She stood beside him silently, chin set with unflagging positivity, enveloping him in that cinnamon-vanilla scent that seemed to get more noticeable with each passing minute. He wanted to mingle that scent with his own, drag her down onto a flat surface and smell every inch of her skin to determine where it radiated from the strongest. Then…God, *then*…he wanted to hear several screamed apologies, back to back, for making his cock hurt so badly.

You can't do it. Remember the damage you've caused.

The clerk cut off his disturbing thoughts by handing him back his credit card. He stared at Sasha the entire time. "All set for room number fourteen."

She smiled. "Thanks. Is there somewhere to eat around here?"

"Not within walking distance, I'm afraid." His hands moved furiously over his desk before handing her a stack of glossy, colorful menus. "Lots of takeout choices. Or I could take you to pick you up something. I get off in—"

"Thanks, we'll manage," Matt interrupted. Apparently the clerk was as slow as his computer. Putting his hand on the small of Lucy's back, he led her out of the office. A glance at a mounted blue sign had him turning right. "If you want something to eat, I'll get it for you."

She held up a Domino's menu with a flourish. "I swore after grad school, I'd never order another Domino's pizza. Didn't even make it one full day."

"I'll let you pick the toppings."

"Oooh. A humorist *and* a gentleman." She grinned up at him, blissfully unaware of his sudden desire to hand-feed her, bite by bite, watching her mouth accept the food he offered. "Be careful or you'll be stuck with me longer than a night."

"Don't jinx me."

"I'm growing on you. I can tell."

Matt bit back a sudden smile. How many times had he been required to do that today? As they walked, his thumb eased under her shirt of its own accord, finding a dimple at the base of her spine. He almost groaned out loud, wishing he could drop to his knees and explore the valley with his mouth. Bumps raised along the skin of her neck as he watched, telling him she felt it, too. It was alarming, how quickly the pulsing need had risen. He could usually keep it leashed until it came time to engage in the actual physical activity. With this girl, his leash had been pulled taut since the moment he laid eyes on her in the coffee shop. Now it threatened to snap. He desperately needed to keep himself in check, for the entire night. But in his current state Matt worried he might not even make it to their room.

He took a deep breath and removed his touch from her skin, wanting to feel the shifting warmth again instantaneously. Green eyes watched him curiously, as if she wanted to say something, but she held out her hand for the key instead. When he followed her inside, it was a struggle not to drag her down to the floor and erase that curiosity once and for all.

Donovan, you're losing it. Reel it back.

Sasha set her purse down on the bed and picked up the telephone. "Pepperoni and black olives?"

He hated black olives. "Your choice." As she placed the order, Matt was painfully aware that he paced the motel room like a starved lion. When she finished her call and flopped back on the bed, he came to a standstill. Jesus, he needed a distraction. Something to keep his mind off her exposed stomach. "So how do you know Lucy?"

She sat up slowly. "Right, Lucy. Um, we met skinny-dipping, actually."

Perfect. Just the distraction he needed. "How's that?"

"A group of my friends sneaked in after hours to the college pool. Illegally, I should add. We thought we were total badasses. Until we walked in and saw Lucy already swimming a naked breast stroke."

Matt felt a tug at the corner of his mouth, even as his body reacted to the image of Sasha, dripping wet, emerging from a pool. "Sounds like the Lucy I've heard about."

In what seemed like an absent gesture, she ran a hand over the comforter. "How come you've never met her? From what Lucy told me, it sounds like you've been friends with her brother for a while."

He leaned back against the table and crossed his arms. "I'm not big on family barbecues."

"No sightseeing, no barbecues. Are you sure you're American?"

This girl made him want to smile and snarl all at the same time. If that had ever happened before, he sure as hell couldn't recall it. Since her question didn't require an answer, he used the opportunity to ask something that had been weighing on his mind since his car had broken down. "Where am I dropping you off tomorrow?"

A long pause. "What do you mean?"

"I mean, when we reach the city, who are you staying with?"

"A friend," she answered too quickly.

Something dense and dangerous settled in Matt's belly. The arrival of jealousy was unwelcome and inappropriate. They didn't have a relationship beyond driver and passenger. He knew that, but rationalizing with the feeling didn't make it go away. "Male or female?"

"Marsupial."

"Sasha."

She visibly winced and the feeling only increased. This girl he was lusting after, feeling territorial over, had a boyfriend. "Female," she answered finally. Matt wasn't sure he believed her, but her softly spoken word calmed him relatively. At least enough to keep at bay the images of her with another man. *Delivering* her to that other man.

He nodded toward the remote control attached to the bedside table with Velcro. "Why don't you find something to watch? I'm going to rinse off." *In the ice-cold shower.*

Looking relieved that he hadn't pursued the subject of where she'd be staying, she nodded, flipping on the television as he passed. Matt walked into the bathroom, turned on the light, and pressed his forehead against the door. Without hesitation, he dropped his hand to the front of his jeans to massage his weighty erection. He had to bite his lip to keep from moaning. Since he'd walked into the damn coffee shop, he'd needed to relieve the pressure and now he'd finally get his chance. He couldn't stop himself from picturing Sasha's teacup-sized breasts. The way her nipples had beaded in the air-conditioning of his car. The pale smoothness of her inner thighs. How he'd like to mark them with his teeth.

When he heard a gasp, followed by a groan, outside the bathroom door, it took Matt a moment to realize the sound hadn't come from his fevered imagination. He held his breath and listened, frowning when he heard it again. Before he even registered his own movement, his hand closed around the doorknob and flung the bathroom door open.

Sasha squealed and dropped the remote control like it was on fire. He realized then, the sounds were coming from the television. A man and a woman, in the throes of orgasm, writhed and bucked on a four-poster bed, cheap art hanging in the background. Porn? She was watching porn?

He pinned Sasha with a look, but she was too busy searching for the remote underneath the bed, ass pointed straight up in the air. "It was the first channel that came on, I swear." Her voice was muffled, but he could just about make out her rambling words over the screams of ecstasy coming from the television. "And it's the weirdest thing because I don't even *watch* porn, but it came up this morning over coffee with a friend. Crazy how things work, isn't it? No porn for years, not a hint of it, then *bam*, it's everywhere."

Matt stood very still, trying his best to find humor in the situation, because she was so clearly lying. Porn definitely got her motor running. But at the end of the day, he was a man. When a gorgeous girl in jean shorts is waving her ass at you, an ass that has been haunting you *all day*, against a backdrop of moaning and slapping flesh, any attempt at maintaining control is compromised. Desire, thick and urgent, arm wrestled with his willpower as his feet started to move. Toward her? Toward the door? He didn't know.

Finally, she sat up on her knees, face flushed from embarrassment and exertion. Her lips were parted and chewed-on. Beautiful. So fucking beautiful. And clean. He shouldn't.

With his control hanging by a string, Matt strode for the door. Just before he reached it, he felt her push up behind him. Hand frozen on the knob, he sucked in a breath as her hands coasted over his ribs and ran up his pectorals with just enough pressure to make his eyes close.

"Don't go," she whispered.

The leash inside him snapped.

...

Lucy's breath got trapped in her lungs when Matt reversed their positions and threw her up against the door. It shook behind her on its hinges, but she didn't feel any pain or alarm. How could she when the man in front of her captured every ounce of her focus? When she'd looked up at him from her kneeling position between the beds, she'd been startled by his expression. Torment had greeted her and she'd known that somehow *she* was partly responsible. He'd wanted her, too. There had been no mistaking that, thanks to the unmistakable bulge behind his partially unbuttoned jeans, his dilated pupils. She could feel his arousal now, rigid against her belly. He pressed their bodies together, head to toe, his mouth drawing oxygen from hers. Her wrists were manacled by his hands, held against the door at her sides.

Between her thighs, dampness spread. This incredible show of dominance...she liked it. A lot. It was what she'd been sensing under his cool surface all day, even if she hadn't recognized it at the time. It's what she'd been responding to in the coffee shop, during the drive. What she'd unconsciously been craving since they'd locked eyes that afternoon. Possibly even before.

Layered beneath the longing, the overwhelming stretch and buildup in her stomach, existed a need to calm whatever she'd seen raging inside him. It felt like a responsibility. One she wanted. One she'd be damned if anyone else got before her.

She attempted to search Matt's eyes, but they were closed tight, the lines between his eyebrows deeply furrowed. His body felt ruthlessly taut, like the string of a guitar. All his strength, held back with firm resolve. "Matt, what's wrong?"

"What's wrong?" he repeated, his lips moving hers as he spoke. "I want to turn you the *fuck* out. That's what's wrong, baby."

Her exhale came out sounding like a moan. She'd known he desired her, but hearing just how much she'd turned him on was a potent aphrodisiac. His voice had taken on a new, rougher quality, crumbling the final illusion of calm, collected Matt. This Matt wanted to take her. Hard. But for some reason, he didn't *want* to want that. Why? "No objections here. I want that, too."

"You don't." He dropped an openmouthed kiss onto the curve of her neck. When she whimpered her enjoyment, it turned into a bite. "You don't know what that means. Not with me."

She was going to lose him if she didn't act. Her hands were immobile, held tightly in his grip, her body flattened so completely against the door, she couldn't move her hips. Taking a deep breath, she leaned forward and bit his ear, tugging it hard. His growl sent shock waves through every corner of her system. "Show me, then."

In one swift motion, he curled his hands around her knees and yanked her legs up to circle his waist. "Squeeze your thighs around me—*tight*—or I'll put you over my knee."

Lucy felt every vital muscle below her waist clench. Holy hell. What had she managed to coax to life inside this man? Why did it excite her more than anything in her recollection? She thought she understood what he meant, but wanted, *needed*, to hear him say the words. "Why would you do that?"

"Because," Matt enunciated, "I want to pleasure your sick little body. I want to make you scream and shake and lose your fucking mind." He surged up between her legs. "But before that, I want to erase any doubt as to who is about to take ownership of you, good girl. Have I scared the hell out of you yet?"

Oh, God. A little. Not enough to want to stop, though. "No."

"Liar. You know what I do to liars?"

"Kiss them?"

"You want to be kissed?"

Lucy nodded eagerly, her gaze dropping to his mouth. More than anything in the world.

Matt licked his lips. "You going to rub that tongue against mine and turn me into a madman? Be ready to drive yourself crazy in the process."

"I'm ready for anything." She held her breath as he leaned in slowly, all that wild intensity focused on her mouth. Back and forth, he rubbed their lips together, tasting her in small, sampling licks and bites. Her eyelids refused to support themselves even as she struggled to keep them up, to watch him. As if each bite of his teeth was injecting her with venom. Not the poisonous kind, though. The kind that attuned every cell in your body to whoever had administered it. *Matt.*

Finally, blessedly, he swept his tongue into her mouth, groaning and pressing closer as he did so. Then he quite simply melted every bone in her body. He released one of her hands to tug down her chin, tilting his head to make as much contact as possible. Their mouths melded together eagerly, tongues seeking and brushing. He was huge between her thighs and she used every bit of mobility she had to grind into him, while kissing him past the point where she needed to draw breath. Pulling away to suck in oxygen didn't seem worth it.

Matt released her mouth, but stayed close as they drew breath. "Did that feel nice? You like the way I kiss your sexy mouth?"

"Yes."

"The sting of my hand wouldn't feel nice. Not the way you want."

"How do you know what I want?" He didn't answer, just took another long pull off her mouth. He shook his head as he did it, as though he was battling some inner demon she couldn't see. "Where do you want to...make it sting, Matt?"

Conflicted eyes shot to hers, causing her heartbeat to falter. His jaw clenched but he said nothing. She took his hand from her chin and kissed his knuckles. In the absence of the light pressure, she realized she'd liked it. "Show me where."

With a tortured growl, both hands cupped her bottom and jerked her against him. At the same time, he bit down on her shoulder, just beside the strap of her tank top. "Please, don't let me do it, baby."

Her mind raced, along with her overloaded senses. She couldn't think of anything but the truth. "Saying things like that only makes me want it more."

"Fuck. *Fuck*." Her words had pushed him past his breaking point. In a blur of motion, he dropped her legs from around his waist and spun her toward the door. "Palms flat on the door. Don't move unless you've been instructed. Is that understood?"

She nodded, unable to force words out of her constricted throat. Her pulse raced like crazy, excitement blooming in every erogenous zone of her body. It occurred to her that someone with a little more common sense might be scared of this particular unknown. Being struck, willingly, by a man she'd just met. Not Lucy. She raced toward the experience with open arms, the thrill seeker she'd buried two years ago doing cartwheels in her belly. *Bring it*.

A gasp slipped past her lips when he fell to his knees and tore the jean shorts down her legs. His shaking hands and labored breathing added a new layer to the thrill. This darkly passionate man wanted her so badly he shook. She wanted to ease the ache she knew he felt. Felt the answering ache inside herself. His pleasure was equally important as her own.

"While we were driving, your ass kept squirming around in the seat. Never fucking stopped. Not for a minute." She cried out when his teeth scraped over her flesh. "Someone needs to hold you still. Someone needs to give you a reason to move that ass around."

One of Matt's fingers slipped under the material of her thong and traced the valley of her bottom before cupping her sex from behind. A whimper broke from her throat as she pictured him crouched down with his hand between her legs, eye level with her bottom. The image, combined with his touch, made a rush of liquid gather under his massaging hand.

He pressed the heel of his hand tight against her core. "That good-girl body gets wet nice and fast, doesn't it? Maybe you're not such a good girl, after all." Through her panties, he pushed his thumb against her clit and twisted it in a circle. She laid her forehead against the door, clutching the cool surface for support. "I know the best way to find out."

"Do it," she pleaded.

He swatted the underside of her bottom, making her cry out, eyes flying open to stare at the door but seeing nothing. Exhilaration raced across her skin, concentrated on the spot his palm had connected with her flesh. The sting had dissipated too quickly and she wanted it back. Bracing herself against the door, she tilted her backside in a silent request for more. Matt was suddenly standing behind her, flush against her back. His stubbled jaw scraped over the hypersensitive skin of her neck, big hand petting her bottom like a precious object.

"Jesus. You're begging me for it, aren't you?" he rasped at her ear, wrapping her hair around his fist and tugging her head back. "Beg harder."

"More, Matt. *Please.*"

He obliged her broken request with another, harder spank of her bottom. She didn't know which one of them made the strangled noise that followed. Maybe they both did. She'd grown so incredibly damp between her thighs that her legs slipped against each other when she attempted to squeeze them together. Barely conscious of her actions now, she pushed her bottom into his hands, shuddering as he slapped her again.

"Hot fucking girl." His palm connected with a firm strike. "Make me hard in public?"

Another strike of his hand. When he once again soothed the spot by stroking it in circles, she shook her head. "S-stop. I like it...the burn."

His hand ceased its movement. "Is that right?"

"*Yes.*"

Rough hands grasped her shoulders and propelled her away from the door. Within seconds, she found herself bent over at the waist, elbows resting on the small dining table placed in the corner of the room. She knew what was coming and braced herself for it. Any second now he would spank her harder than before, no holding back. She couldn't wait. Wanted it so bad.

A knock sounded at the door. "Pizza delivery."

For long, torturous seconds, neither one of them moved. No sounds could be heard in the room save their harsh breathing. *Oh God, he's going to stop. No, no—*

Slap.

Lucy screamed.

Chapter Four

When Sasha screamed his name, Matt slipped a little closer toward insanity. Who the hell *was* this girl? What was she doing to him?

He'd heard the knock on the door, knew the right thing to do would be to answer it, pay the man and end what he'd unwisely started with her. If he wasn't careful, he'd become addicted to her. Hell, he might already be halfway there. She hadn't shied away from him, hadn't looked at him with fear or disgust. Only an insatiable need for more. A need that possibly even matched his own. The trust she continued to show him, not holding anything back…it had drawn the very thing out of him he'd worked for years to keep under wraps. He couldn't control it around her. More, she didn't want him to. Christ, she was breathtaking.

When he'd heard another man's voice so close to her, where she'd stood naked and vulnerable, his first instinct hadn't been to cover her up. Or put a stop to what would undoubtedly end with him buried in her sweet body. *No.* His instinct had been to claim her, in a way that any male in the vicinity knew who the fuck she belonged to. It came on so powerful and swift that he couldn't deny it or hold back. So he'd raised his hand and spanked her so hard he could still make out his handprint. He'd wanted her to scream loud enough to shake the rafters. He'd wanted everyone to hear it.

Now, though, he waited, heart beating in his throat. This is where she would scramble for her clothes, crying, shouting through her tears for him to stay away. Any second now she would shatter him. This brave, amazing girl had been willing to trust him and he'd pushed too hard. He'd let his need to touch her block everything else out.

He held his breath as Sasha tossed back her strawberry-blond curls, meeting his eyes over her shoulder. Her lips were damp and parted, eyes smoky. Magnificent. His cock swelled so huge against his belly he had to support himself with a hand on the table. "Again, Matt."

His forehead dropped down onto her back with a groan. *She can't be real.* Part of him wished like hell she hadn't just given him permission to go further, because he'd be incapable of stopping now. This is when his appetite turned dangerous, where the last vestiges of his control went down the drain. She didn't, *couldn't,* know what she was getting into. When another more tentative knock came from the door, she worked her ass in circles on his lap, as if he needed any more encouragement to ignore the intrusion.

Slap. Slap. Her answering moan caused a hot, deep clenching in his belly. He needed to take her now. The need raged inside him like a hurricane. With a twist of his wrist, he ripped the light-pink panties from her body, jaw clenching when she only arched her back. In anticipation? God, he hoped so. Stopping now could very well kill him.

Matt inserted his foot between her ankles and forced her legs wide, then thrust two fingers into her damp opening. *So goddamn tight.*

"You're going to be sore tomorrow. From me. From how I'm about to fuck you. Every time you walk, sit, or stand, you're going to think of me."

"Yes. *Please*. I will."

Ass reddened by his hand, thighs spread in welcome, she had to be the most erotic sight he'd ever laid eyes on. Possession gripped him around the throat as he took the condom from his wallet, unbuttoned his jeans fully and rolled the latex down his sensitive length. He took his cock in his hand and rubbed the head against her clit, savoring the little whimpering noises she made in her throat, watching as her hips began to shake. He started to ease inside her, but something stopped him. It felt too impersonal, taking her this way after the trust she'd shown him. He wanted to look at her, see her face when he entered her for the first time.

Quickly, he turned her, something foreign flooding his chest when he saw her flushed face, her passion-glazed eyes. *Yes*, this is what he wanted. This felt right. She was impatient, too, he realized. Her throaty groan of frustration had Matt dragging her close, stripping her shirt off over her head so he could watch her pink-tipped breasts bounce. Supporting himself on the table with one hand, he hefted her up so she could wrap her legs around his waist.

"Take me deep, Sasha. I can't wait any longer to fuck you. I *need* you."

Something akin to panic flared in her eyes just as he drove into her with a hard upward thrust. "Matt—"

Then it was gone, as though he'd imagined it. Hidden behind her expression of shocked pleasure. His vision swam when he finally managed to shift his hips enough to bury himself to the hilt. Never. He'd never felt anything like her. She squeezed every inch of him like a vise, already beginning to contract, milking him before he'd even moved.

"Oh…oh my God. Matt."

He spoke through clenched teeth. "Tell me when you've gotten used to me."

"N-now. I'm...*now*." Fingernails sinking into his shoulders, she dug her heels into the flesh of his ass and started writhing against his lap in midair. Fuck. He nearly came then and there, just from the sight of her. Head thrown back, lithe body undulating in quick circles designed to short-circuit his brain. Her pussy held him in such a tight grip, he knew her body couldn't have accommodated him so easily, but she kept moving nonetheless, teeth sunk into her bottom lip as if the pressure between her legs were the only conscious part of her world.

Matt took her ass in his hands, lifting her and slamming her back down onto his cock. "You like when it hurts a little, baby?"

Her breath shuddered out. "I-I like the way you do it."

His growl caused her eyes to pop open. Not in fear, but with excitement. It let loose something inside him, something he'd never felt. It took over, commanding his body for him. Before he could register his own actions, he dragged her down onto the floor, flipped her over and entered her from behind. "These thighs were made to be spread for a man. This man. Open them wider. *Now*."

"Yes."

His fingers tangled themselves in her hair, drawing her head back until she cried out. Some untapped part of him craved authority over her, going hand in hand with his dictation of her body's responses. He needed her to recognize it. "Yes, *please*."

"Please!"

Matt drove into her, over and over, the sound of slapping bodies and wild moans filling the room. Her body counteracted each movement of his own perfectly, all wet friction and tight strokes of flesh. He watched as the shaking started in her shoulders and moved down her back. He wanted to make her release powerful, *needed* her to associate pleasure with him for the rest of her life. His fingers traced over her pumping hip to massage her clit, speeding up as her movements grew jerky and desperate.

"I'm...oh, please..."

"Come. *Now.* Let me feel what I did to you." Operating on instinct, he reared back with his hand and slapped her ass. He felt her go over the edge, her inner muscles spasming around him. The feel of her—tight, shaking perfection—sent him growling into his own climax, pumping into her as long as he could. Never wanting it to end. *"Sasha."*

· · ·

Hearing her best friend's name on Matt's lips instead of her own felt like an ice pick lodging itself in Lucy's sternum.

What have I done?

She'd tried to stop him; the words had been poised on her lips just before he entered her. Then he'd filled her so thoroughly and started moving. Stopping him, telling him the truth on the chance he might walk away and leave her cold, hadn't been an option. Not if she wanted to go on breathing. From that point forward, she'd been mindless to anything but his mastering of her body. There simply wasn't another word for it. He'd mastered her completely, breaking her down and making her whole at the same time. It didn't seem possible that she'd only met him this afternoon.

The physical attraction between them was a force in itself. Add to it the foreign mixture of yearning and concern she'd felt for him, this *need* to be exactly what *he* needed...

It was exactly how he was looking at her right now.

He sat back on the carpet and pulled her into his lap, lips tracing over her hair, murmuring words she couldn't afford to discern.

He thinks you're someone else.

"Tell me you're okay."

Lucy nodded vigorously, swallowing the hard knot in her throat. She knew he wanted her to say something, but she couldn't manage words. It felt like someone was choking her. The concern in his voice, the way his fingers drew soothing circles on her hips and stomach, she didn't deserve it. *Liar.* She'd never expected to feel something as powerful as the response he'd drawn from her body. Never expected to feel a connection. How stupid she'd been to assume that anything with this man could be casual. The demons behind his eyes should have been a warning. Her reaction to them should have been a bright, blinking caution sign.

Lucy knew the truth, though. She'd seen the warning signs and gone hurtling past them anyway. It's that lack of restraint that had landed her in trouble countless times. A little voice whispered in her head now, telling her the consequences of tricking him would be far worse than she'd ever experienced in the past.

Without warning, he lifted her into his arms. "What are you doing?"

He didn't answer, continuing his long strides toward the bathroom. When they walked inside, he didn't turn on the fluorescent light, thankfully. She had a feeling her eyes would betray everything. As it was, the soft light filtering in from the bedroom revealed too much. Matt set her on her feet and stood behind her. Their gazes met and what she saw there caused a flood of guilt in her chest. Anxiety tightened his features as he broke their eye contact and began inspecting her body.

He sucked in a breath, running gentle hands over her bottom. "Baby."

"It doesn't hurt," she managed. That was only half a lie,

but it still felt bitter on her tongue. Were lies going to come so easy to her now that she'd gotten the ball rolling?

Matt reached around her, his hand closing around a minuscule bottle of complimentary lotion with the motel's logo printed on the side. It took his unscrewing the cap to discern his intention. "It's not much, but it will help with the redness."

Lucy tried to turn and stop him, but when coolness replaced the raw sting on her skin, her mouth snapped shut. Until that moment, she hadn't realized exactly how sore the spanking had left her. Instead of alarming, she found her condition…thrilling. Watching him in the mirror, seeing him attend to her so diligently, made her feel powerful. Cherished.

What an odd reaction. Yet there it was. The same feeling she'd had against the door, bent over the table, kneeling on the floor. It didn't make sense, since Matt had been holding the reins, commanding her, dominating her. Somehow, she'd never felt so in control.

Lips tracing across her bare shoulder distracted her. As if on cue, her head tilted to the side, encouraging him. "We should have had a safe word," he said. "I didn't know it would get that far. I'm so sorry."

"Safe word," she repeated, searching her brain for where she'd heard that term before. Sasha, maybe. Or in a book. "It's okay. I wouldn't have used it."

Matt exhaled in a rush, meeting her eyes again as he continued massaging her bottom in gentle circles. She felt herself go a little light-headed. The image of this absurdly masculine man behind her, treating her with such care, would surely be imprinted on her brain for the rest of her life. Tall as he was, she could feel his abdomen pressed against her back, his strong thighs flush with her naked bottom. The cut muscles in his arms flexed as he applied the lotion, eyes watching her with such intensity in the mirror, seeming to glow.

She thought back to his fervent words, when this whole thing had started. *Don't let me do it… Have I scared the hell out of you yet?* Again, the need to soothe him rose like a tide. The way he was looking at her, as if worried he'd broken her…she couldn't let him continue to think that way. She'd loved everything they'd done. God, she wanted to do it again. As in, *now.* Would have already suggested it if it were possible. But her lie had damned her. She couldn't be with him again, her inexcusable deception hanging over her head. Still, she couldn't leave him with any doubt that he'd given her incredible pleasure.

Lucy turned, gasping when his erection slid across her belly. He'd been holding himself away from her, so she wouldn't feel it. For some reason, that bothered the hell out of her. She'd just resolved to distance herself from him before she made her dishonest actions even worse, but standing this close to him, seeing that disquiet in his eyes, it flattened her resolve like a pancake. Of its own accord, her fingers traced over the ridges of his abs, watching in fascination as his chest began to rise and fall faster.

"Matt—"

A knock at the door. Matt cursed.

Her eyebrows rose. "That is one persistent pizza delivery guy."

The corners of his mouth lifted even as he shook his head. "Stay here. I'll go pay for it." He went to leave the bathroom, then turned back and dropped a sweet, slow kiss on her mouth. When he pulled away, he backed out of the bathroom as if afraid to lose sight of her. That look caused something awful to coil uncomfortably inside of her. He didn't know who he was looking at in such a manner. He thought she was someone else entirely. Not the impulsive idiot she was in reality. *Dammit to hell, Lucy.*

She turned and stared at her reflection in the mirror. Hair a tumbled mess, lips swollen, she barely recognized herself. It was more than her appearance, though. The regret coursing through her veins was palpable in the air around her. After a moment, she overheard snippets of the discussion taking place at the door.

Found the part after all...installed...car's ready to go...

Relief and disappointment warred so hard in her stomach, it caused her eyes to close. Leaving now and continuing their drive to New York meant she wouldn't have to face her lie much longer. She could part ways with him, hope he would chalk their encounter up to a hot fling and not pursue seeing her again. The crippling wave of panic that came along with that thought, however, blocked everything else out. She should come clean. Now. Before another minute passed.

And see the tenderness in his eyes turn to disgust?

No. Maybe it made her a coward, but she couldn't do it. Just a few more hours and she could leave him with a fond memory, instead of the outrage she suspected would come along with finding out she was Brent's little sister.

Outside the bathroom, she heard the door close. Taking a deep breath for courage, she pasted a smile on her face and walked out into the bedroom to find him, hands on hips, staring thoughtfully at the door. He snapped to attention when he saw her, but looked less than pleased.

"The car is re—"

"I heard," Lucy interrupted brightly. "That's great news."

"Is it?" Matt said under his breath. Swallowing hard, Lucy pretended not to hear him as she pulled on her clothes, doing her best not to wince when the material dragged over her sensitive backside.

When she'd finished dressing and he still hadn't moved, she had no choice but to face him. There was no way to prevent her eyes from tracking down over his shirtless body.

Good Lord, he enlivened every cell in her body. Knowing she could never allow herself to touch him again caused her physical pain. "What?"

"You seem awfully eager to leave."

Lucy steeled herself against the urge to drop her purse and throw herself into his arms. Instead, she waggled her eyebrows. "I've got big plans for this week. I guess I'm eager to get started."

Then without a backward glance, she breezed out of the room and headed in the direction of the garage, hating herself a little more every step of the way.

Chapter Five

Matt's hands clenched on the steering wheel as he exited the Holland Tunnel. Minutes away from dropping Sasha off and he still had no idea where the hell they stood. She'd been feigning sleep for the last fifty miles, head propped against the window, her curls still messy from his goddamn hands. Several times he'd had to tamp down the urge to pull over and drag her across the console onto his lap. Not to fuck her, although that's undoubtedly where it would lead if he got that close. First, though, he wanted to get an honest reaction out of her. If it meant interrogating her on the side of the highway, he'd been prepared to do just that.

Then the flashbacks had started, causing him to question everything. Had he imagined her enthusiasm when they'd made love back in the motel room? Had her uninhibited response been a projection, something he'd wanted to see, but didn't really exist? It stood to reason, since she'd been deathly quiet afterward, standing motionless in front of him in the bathroom, pale as a ghost. God, if he'd hurt her...

Matt glanced at her delicate form for what felt like the

thousandth time. Shit, he'd been rough as hell with her. She'd seemed to want it, even requested it. Hadn't she? He'd been so fucking gone for her, bursting at the seams with lust and the need to please her, he wondered now if that had shaded his perception. His needs had been kept locked up so tight for so damn long. Sweated out of him nightly as he went round after round with the punching bag that hung suspended in his apartment. He hadn't been prepared for her. Hadn't had time to bring the urges down from a boiling point to the slow simmer he walked around with each day.

He came to a stop at a red light just as another unwelcome image assailed him. A familiar woman, forcibly pushing him away, eyes filled with disgust. *Get away from me. What is wrong with you? I don't even know you anymore, Matt.*

Unease clogged his throat. Had he missed the signs with Sasha? Even worse, had he…ignored them? It had been so damn long since he'd allowed that side of him to surface, maybe he'd been too overcome with need to recognize that she'd wanted him to stop. What other explanation could there be for her sudden urgency to leave? If he'd had his way, they would still be in that motel room. He'd be fucking her in the shower, on the bed, on any available surface he could find. He sure as shit wouldn't be getting ready to drop her off at a fucking Starbucks in Midtown.

As soon as they'd gotten on the road, her plan had changed. She'd texted a "friend" who apparently thought it was easier if they met at yet another coffee shop. This friend thought their apartment would be too hard for them to find. He hadn't bought it. He didn't want to drop her off at all, but if he was being forced to leave her somewhere, he wanted to see her there safely.

Maybe she's scared of you and doesn't want you to know where she's staying.

Matt swallowed that disturbing thought, hoping it wasn't true. The light turned green and he eased off the brake. He wanted to see her again. Hell, he *needed* to. If only to make up for taking her from behind on the floor of a motel room. She deserved better than that. He wanted to be the one who gave it to her. Had he blown his only chance? This couldn't be the last time he laid eyes on her. The very notion of their association ending in mere minutes felt undeniably wrong.

Up ahead, the Starbucks came into view and he barely resisted the impulse to keep driving. All the way to his downtown apartment. How would she react? *Not well*, he thought, wryly. As much as she'd surrendered to him that afternoon, she was full of fire. Not the type to take lightly a man changing her plans without consulting her.

With a brick in his stomach, Matt pulled his car to a stop outside the Starbucks. Right on cue, Sasha opened her eyes and gave an exaggerated stretch. "Good timing," he said.

She blinked innocently. "W-where are we?"

Right. He sighed and climbed out of the car to retrieve her suitcase, all the while trying to figure out how to convince her to give him another chance. He could see her rounding the car through the back windshield, could see her nervous expression. Already, he could practically feel her slipping out of his reach. *You did this. It's your fault she can't wait to get away from you.*

The second Sasha reached him, she curled her hand under the handle of the suitcase. "Thank you. I, um…appreciate the ride."

It was right on the tip of his tongue to tell her he wasn't leaving. That he wouldn't just drop her off in the middle of New York City and drive away. That it felt unnatural to leave her, *period*. But she continued to avoid his gaze, shifting nervously like she might break out into a sprint at any minute. It was worse than he'd anticipated. If he insisted on staying with her, it could increase the damage he'd already done.

Having no other choice, Matt reached into the still-open trunk and retrieved his police notepad from the duffel bag he kept stored there. As she watched wide-eyed, he wrote his phone number down on a piece of paper and handed it to her. He knew if he asked for hers, she would balk. This would not be the last time he saw her, though. If it meant biting the bullet and asking Brent to get her number from Lucy, he would do it. Even if it meant handing his friend enough material to torture him with for years. She was worth it.

"If you need anything, you call me. *Anything.*" Unable to resist, he took a step closer, letting his fingers trace down the side of her face. Did her lower lip tremble of out fear or something else? "I don't like this."

"What?" she whispered.

"Not knowing where you'll be. Who you'll be with."

She looked to the side. "You're not responsible for me."

His thumb brushed her lip. Fuck it. He couldn't hold anything back with his girl. "Maybe I want to be. Use my number, Sasha."

Her eyes squeezed shut and she visibly shook herself, as if he'd said something to break the spell. "Matt, look. I appreciate the ride, but I have to go."

Reluctantly, he let his hand drop. "Use my number."

She didn't reply.

He watched as she wheeled her suitcase into the Starbucks, vanishing from his sight. For long moments, he couldn't get his legs to move, but finally managed to get into his car and pull away from the curb. If he felt like he'd forgotten something, it was because he had. Briefly. Now, as he drove alone, farther away from her, he remembered what it was.

Alone was the best place for him.

• • •

Lucy bought a cup of coffee and waited for Matt's car to leave, drinking deeply of the hot, black liquid to keep herself from running after him. Telling him everything. The way he'd looked at her when they parted ways...it had left her feeling hollow inside. When he finally left, she sat rooted to her chair for long minutes, staring at nothing, before pulling her cell phone out of her shorts pocket. After a minute of debate, she dialed Hayden.

Her brother's fiancée answered on the second ring, sounding surprised. "Lucy?"

"Hey."

A brief pause. "Where are you and Sasha? I thought you'd be here by now."

She meant Brent's house in Queens, where Matt *would* have dropped her off, if he'd known she was actually Lucy. If she didn't have a strict budget to get her through the week, she would have walked outside and hailed a cab to Brent's place. But as it was, she'd already be scraping by without springing for the extra thirty dollars. "I had a...change of plans. I'm at a Starbucks in Manhattan. And it's just me. Sasha couldn't make it." She blew out a breath. "Listen, I wouldn't ask for a ride unless I really needed it—"

"Say no more. I'll call Brent and let him know—"

"Actually, do you mind keeping this between us?" She didn't want to get Matt in trouble with her brother when he'd done nothing wrong. "Just for now?"

A brief pause. "Text me the address. I'm on the way."

Half an hour later, Lucy watched Hayden double-park her silver Lexus and step out onto the sidewalk. *Wow.* Lucy had gathered, based on Brent's description, that Hayden was a stunner, but she hadn't been prepared for the polar opposite of her brash, ball-breaking brother to show up. Polished and put-together, she practically radiated her upper-crust upbringing.

Lucy tossed her empty coffee cup in the trash and wheeled her suitcase outside to join her, feeling more than a little self-conscious in her cutoff shorts and hair that looked like it had been put through a weed whacker. When she noticed Hayden wringing her hands, clearly just as nervous for their first meeting, she was put immediately at ease.

"The prodigal daughter has returned."

Hayden smiled warmly. "Lucy."

They hesitated, then hugged a little awkwardly. "Sorry to bring you all the way out here."

"Not a problem. Brent had to work a late shift tonight, so I was just catching up on some paperwork. Anyway, I've been told to expect the unexpected with you."

When Hayden popped the trunk, Lucy heaved her suitcase inside, ignoring the sting that came along with the good-natured remark. "It's true. I like to keep everyone on their toes."

Seconds later, they pulled into traffic and were heading uptown. After living in Syracuse so long, being in Manhattan felt like she'd landed on a different planet. Lights, sounds, rumbling, shouting, movement. It didn't make her nervous, though. Anticipation and a curl excitement filled a little bit of the hole the afternoon had left inside her, but not nearly enough to forget Matt's face as she walked away. *Think of something else.*

"So, Hayden. If you don't mind me asking…?"

"Fire away."

"How did my brother manage to land you?"

Hayden's laugh bounced around the interior of the car. "I assure you, I landed *him*."

Lucy considered the brunette, heard the sincerity ringing in her voice, and nodded. "Nice pull, Brent," she murmured, staring back through the windshield.

"Since we're asking questions," Hayden began hesitantly, "do you want to tell me why Matt dropped you off in the wrong place? That's not like him. He's normally very…regimented."

Something about the car's dark interior and the exhaustion that suddenly came over her had tears threatening behind Lucy's eyes. The need to unburden herself, if just partially, couldn't be denied. "I screwed up," she whispered. "Matt didn't do anything wrong."

Hayden didn't say anything for a moment. "Do you want to tell me about it?"

Lucy could only shake her head. When Hayden turned off Riverside Drive and coasted to a stop in front of a town house, Lucy glanced at her questioningly. "Where are we?"

"This is my place." She sounded almost embarrassed over that fact, but Lucy couldn't fathom why. "For another couple weeks, anyway. I'm handing over the keys to the new owner in July when I permanently move in with Brent." Her face flushed a little. "When I thought you were bringing a friend along for the week, I thought you could make use of it. You know, two single girls in Manhattan, so close to the action…"

For a girl who grew up sharing everything with two gigantic older brothers, then stuffed into a dorm, followed by a tiny two-bedroom for the last six years, the very idea floored her. She just barely resisted the urge to cabbage patch. "Me? This place?"

"That *was* the idea, but now that you're solo—"

"Even better. I don't have to wear pants."

Hayden nodded sagely. "There is that."

Lucy pushed the passenger-side door open and stood, staring up at the town house. Hayden rounded the car to stand beside her. "Thanks, Hayden. I really appreciate this."

"Sure." She shifted in her high heels. "I hope it doesn't seem like we don't want you with us in Queens. Brent wasn't exactly thrilled when I suggested this. He was looking forward to having his sister around."

Something lodged in Lucy's throat. "Really?" she managed.

Bafflement transformed Hayden's features. "Of course."

What would he think if he knew you'd duped his best friend into sleeping with you?

With that disturbing thought ringing in her head, Lucy busied herself removing her suitcase from the trunk. Hayden put a hand on her wrist to stop her. "Wait. I figured you would stay with us, at least for tonight. You probably haven't even eaten—"

"Really, I'm just exhausted. I wouldn't be good company." Lucy kept her smile in place, but it felt like it might crack at any moment. "I can order takeout or something. Don't worry about me."

Hayden looked dubious, but stepped back. "I guess we'll see you tomorrow night, no matter what, right?"

Lucy pulled the handle up on her suitcase. "Tomorrow night?"

"Brent didn't tell you?" At Lucy's blank expression, she sighed. "My parents are throwing us an engagement party at their place, which is actually right around the corner from here. It's going to be small. Mostly just family and a few close friends." She twisted her engagement ring on her finger. "You'll come, won't you?"

Close friends. Oh God, would Matt be there? The blood in Lucy's veins froze, but she couldn't deny a tiny flip in her stomach that she would see him again, no matter the circumstances. Proving she needed a psychiatric evaluation stat. There was no way she could avoid her brother's engagement party, though. She no longer had school as an excuse. Hayden stood there, watching her expectantly, raising a perfectly plucked eyebrow when Lucy stayed silent far too long. Obviously, she would have to go and pray Matt didn't attend. Or…hide when he did?

The live studio audience in her head broke into laughter, at her expense.

She cleared her throat. "Wouldn't miss it."

Chapter Six

Matt stood outside the Upper West Side brownstone, debating whether or not to actually go inside. *Small get-together*, Brent had told him. Right. It looked like half the city was in attendance. He wasn't good with crowds and even worse making small talk. This was not his scene, a fact Brent obviously knew well, hence his under-exaggeration. After the sleepless night he'd had after dropping off Sasha, he was even less equipped than usual to handle this many people, closing in on him, making him feel claustrophobic.

Parties had never appealed to him, but since returning from Afghanistan, they made him even more uncomfortable. He couldn't monitor everything taking place around him, couldn't see who was standing behind him, didn't like the constant coming and going of new faces. It made him sweat, made it harder to focus on the questions people inevitably threw at him after a few drinks. *What did you do, exactly, overseas? Did you see action? Is* The Hurt Locker *an accurate portrayal?*

It brought the memories he lived with each day even

closer to the surface, until they were unavoidable. Until he couldn't blink without seeing the horror all over again, feel the sun beating down on him as he waited for a target to move into place. Sometimes he could even taste the sand in his mouth, feel it in his eyes. They all paled in comparison to the worst memory of all, the one that felt fresh enough to have occurred yesterday.

Tommy.

The front door of the brownstone burst open, interrupting his thoughts. Brent ducked under the doorframe and walked out onto the top step. "You going to stand out here all night, Matty? We got free food in here. Don't make me come down there and put you in a headlock."

Despite his reluctance to go inside, he felt himself relax. He had a love-hate relationship with Brent, but he knew his friends were the only thing keeping him from the total seclusion he craved. Being a sniper condoned his isolation, in a way. Thankfully, they never pried too far into his past, something for which he was grateful. Even so, they'd made it clear that when he felt like talking about it, they would listen.

He'd had people in his life once before like that, though, hadn't he? Before the rug got pulled out from under him, leaving him flat on his ass.

Brent made an impatient noise. "Come on, sweetheart. I promise I'll be with you the whole time."

Matt casually flipped him the bird as he ascended the steps.

"That's more like it. Let's get you a cold one." Brent threw a heavy arm around his shoulder. "There are a bunch of dudes with trays, handing out pink champagne. If I'm not careful I'm going to start liking it. If that ever happens, take my man card, please."

"You lost your man card when you belted the *Beaches* theme song at City Hall."

They walked inside, Brent immediately zeroing in on Hayden, who turned and met his eyes on cue. "Yeah. But look what I got in exchange."

Matt declined a glass of champagne with a shake of his head. "So what happened to this being a small get-together?"

Brent shrugged and took the champagne Matt had declined. "You know how the Winsteads roll. I think I saw Donald Trump around here somewhere." He downed the drink in one gulp. "Hey, man. Did I thank you yet for getting Lucy here in one piece? That's no small accomplishment. She usually leaves some form of destruction in her path. I guess she's like her brother in that way."

"Lucy?" Matt shook his head "She's with her boyfriend at his lake house."

Brent leaned back. "Lucy has a boyfriend?" He set the empty glass down with a decisive *thunk*. "My little *sister* has a boyfriend?"

Hayden walked up and laid a hand on Brent's arm. "Everything okay here, gents?"

"Where'd Lucy go?" Brent scanned the crowd. "Apparently there's some guy with a lake house I need to put the fear of God into."

Matt held up a hand. "Wait. Lucy is here?"

Brent tilted his head. "Have you been stealing pot from the evidence locker again? You dropped her off here last night."

He opened his mouth to correct Brent when he saw her. The words died on his lips, along with any semblance of rational thought. Sasha. In a strapless green dress, tipping back a glass of champagne as she walked in his direction. His body's reaction was twice as potent as the day in the coffee shop because this time, he knew. Knew she could turn him inside out with a look, a touch, a sound ripped from her throat. She was danger on two legs and he wanted to immerse himself in it. Her.

These fevered thoughts came and multiplied in strength before she'd even noticed him standing there, but now she slowed to a stop, gaze shooting wide. Steps faltering. As if she'd never expected to see him again. Oh, he didn't fucking like that at all. Matt allowed the satisfying image of him carrying her from the party over his shoulder to linger in his mind. It made up for her lack of pleasure at discovering him there. He'd thought of her nonstop since last night, worrying for her safety, wondering if he'd hurt her, fantasizing about their too-short hour in the motel, when she'd obviously had no intention of calling him.

"Luce, get over here." Brent dragged her forward and held her against his side. "You have a boyfriend and you didn't tell me?"

Matt felt the blood drain from his face. No...no. Please let him have heard wrong. Sasha wasn't Sasha...she was Lucy? Lucy, as in Brent's sister. How could it be possible? Seeing her petite form standing beside Brent, such a huge contrast in their appearances, made it seem like a crazy joke. But it so obviously wasn't. Her guilt was plastered all over her face. Not happening. Jesus. This girl, whom he'd had one of the most honest experiences of his life with, had been lying to him the whole time. It felt like déjà vu.

She'd made him a fool. Again.

Lucy gave a barely perceptible head shake, and what he interpreted as an apology with her eyes, but he was beyond caring. Still, he couldn't quite bring himself to walk away yet. Worse, far worse, he still wanted her, dammit. That burned most of all.

"Who told you I had a boyfriend?" she asked Brent, still watching him closely.

"Your chauffer, Matt, ratted you out."

She laughed, a hint of humor making her green eyes

twinkle. It was such a Brent-like characteristic, Matt wanted to kick himself for not seeing it before. *You were too focused on the rest of her, though, weren't you?* "You know Matt. Joke a minute. Halfway here yesterday, I started calling him Chuckles."

"Damn, I should have thought of that."

Out of the corner of his eye, Matt noticed Hayden scrutinizing him and realized he hadn't even attempted to hide his reaction to seeing Lucy. Brent seemed a little too high on life to notice, but his shocked silence hadn't escaped Hayden, obviously. Right now, he had a decision to make. The right thing would be to come clean, tell his best friend what went down, leaving out all of the graphic details. Yet everything inside him rebelled at the notion. He couldn't look his best friend in the eye and tell him he screwed his little sister on the floor of a cheap motel room.

A wave of dizziness swept through Matt as the magnitude of that hit home. He'd done more than screw her brains out, he'd laid his hands on her. Hard. Left marks.

No, he couldn't do it. How would he ever look Brent in the face ever again?

"Oh hey, Luce." Brent nudged his sister, who continued to look pale. "You know what I found in the basement last week?"

"Not a clue."

"Your accordion."

She choked on a sip of her drink. "Please tell me you burned it."

"Ever better." He winked. "I brought it with me tonight."

"Can't imagine why," Lucy snorted.

"Oh, I think you know why. You're playing it."

"When hell freezes over."

Brent shivered. "Is it getting cold in here?"

• • •

You have got to be fucking kidding me.

When the crowd had parted and she'd seen Matt, looking gorgeous and uncomfortable all at the same time, she'd thought *this is going to be the worst night of my life.*

She'd had no idea.

How her brother had managed to convince her to play an accordion in front of these coolly sophisticated Manhattanites, she would never fully understand. At first, he'd made the request by calling her performance an engagement gift. When she'd still balked, he'd led every guest in the vicinity in chanting her name until she'd had no choice but to take the offered instrument and give in. And maybe, just maybe, a tiny part of her wanted to escape Matt's blazing stare.

She couldn't afford to think about it now. Or the hurt she'd glimpsed just before he put his mask back in place. A hundred pairs of eyes were trained on her. Palms sweating, knees shaking. It was like she'd been transported back to her fourth-grade talent show. She'd practiced for weeks only to be beaten by Becky Kessler's dance routine, performed to Hanson's "MmmBop." When she felt a surge of annoyance over the memory, she realized she'd never really let the defeat go.

Repressed talent show angst. We've reached a new low.

Everyone was waiting for her to say something, but she could only look at Matt. He'd gotten past the hurt and confusion. He was angry now. Good. Better to have him angry. At least she could handle that emotion from him. She was well used to people being angry with her.

She cleared her throat into the silence. "Um…something in French?"

A couple guys in suits gave her a golf clap. Brent whooped

from the back of the crowd, but when Hayden punched him in the arm it ended in a yelp. Eyes closed, Lucy played a few notes on the piano side of the accordion, hoping like hell she remembered the song she had in mind start to finish.

She didn't. Halfway through the lively song about a young French maid losing her virtue in a field, the lyrics completely fled her brain. People were smiling and bobbing their heads at her, though. That was a good sign, right? If she could just make it through the end of the song, she might escape this without requiring ten years' worth of therapy. What were those stupid lyrics? Not a single word came to mind. Praying no one in the room knew French, Lucy started singing about another tragedy, possibly worse than the French maid losing her V-card.

J'ai rencontré un bel homme
Nous sommes allés à l'hôtel
Il a fessé mon cul, notre pizza partit
Et je suis en enfer maintenant.

Which roughly translated to:

I met a lovely fellow
We went to a motel
He spanked my ass
Our pizza left
And now I am in hell.

Lucy winced when a bald man to her left spit out his champagne. Apparently, there was at least one French speaker in the house. Finally, *finally* the song ended and the room broke out into polite applause. As quickly as possible, she set her accordion down on the nearest table, relieved when everyone went back to their conversations fairly quickly. Her eyes immediately sought Matt where he stood near the door.

He was stillness in a room full of movement, gray gaze cutting through the vibrant crowd.

He nodded once, as if he'd made a decision. Then he turned and walked out the front door. Brent and Hayden were having an animated conversation that looked like it would end in them making out, so they didn't notice his exit.

She should let him go. Definitely shouldn't follow him. So why were her feet moving? Maybe she would just explain, issue an apology, and get it off her chest. Perhaps it wouldn't do an ounce of good, possibly could even make things worse, but she couldn't just let him walk out after shocking him the way she had. The thought that he might leave hating her was a decidedly sour one. At the very least she could get some closure on this situation.

Lucy almost laughed. There wouldn't be closure any time soon. Not after what they'd shared. Not a moment had passed since last night that she didn't replay his fervent words against her lips, the hint of torment in his voice. His hands, the way they'd positioned her so commandingly, so he could drive into her with perfect precision.

Decision made, Lucy skirted past a group of women discussing their plan to snag police officers for themselves and darted along the wall, hoping no one saw her. Warm summer breeze greeted her outside, carrying the scent of the Hudson River and a nearby bakery. Descending the steps, she looked right and left, finally catching sight of Matt halfway down the block.

"Matt. Wait."

His shoulders stiffened and he slowed to a stop, but didn't turn around. She kept walking until she stood five feet away, staring nervously at his back.

"What is it, *Lucy*?"

The sharp way he said her name sent a jolt through her, but there was also a sense of relief to finally hear him call her by the correct name. And boy, did *that* make her feel like an asshole. "I just wanted to say I'm sorry. I know that's not even remotely adequate, but I couldn't let you leave without hearing it." He turned slowly and she fell back a step at the anger she saw in his expression, yet still he said nothing. "Could you please say something?"

"Why did you do it? Why lie?"

Stupidly, that was the one question she hadn't anticipated. She'd expected, or *hoped* rather, that he would just shout something awful at her. It would have made her feel better. Absolved her of a tiny bit of her guilt. Instead, he'd caught her off guard, giving her no choice but to answer honestly. "I wanted you. In the coffee shop, before I knew who you were," she said quietly, watching his jaw clench. "Then I heard you call me a nuisance…and I guess I just wanted to be someone who didn't inspire irritation. Just for one day. I didn't want to be your best friend's little sister. I wanted to be me."

"Only you weren't you. You pretended to be someone else."

"The only thing I lied about was my name. Everything else—"

"In this case, your name was the most important detail." He pushed a hand through his black hair. "I never would have touched you if I'd known."

"That's the other reason I lied," she whispered, trying to ignore the stab of hurt over his statement. She didn't want to hear that. Wanted to keep imagining that he'd been so attracted to her that he'd had no choice.

Eyes closed, Matt shook his head. "It can't happen again. It *won't*." He stepped closer and lowered his voice. "I fucked you on your hands and knees on the floor of a dingy motel room that rented by the hour. More than that, I—"

"Spanked me. Manhandled me." She didn't know where the words came from, only knew that now that they'd been spoken, the air thickened between her and Matt. In the space of seconds, her breath had grown shallow, cheeks flaming. She might have stopped there, but Matt's chest shuddered and she couldn't hold back the truth. "I liked it, Matt."

"*Stop.*" He stepped even closer, contradicting his harsh command. As though he couldn't help himself, his gaze dropped to her breasts where, thanks to her excitement, they swelled at the top of her dress. "It doesn't matter. Now that I know who you are, touching you would be inexcusable."

"But you want to."

He sucked in a breath. "Lucy, that's *enough.*"

The authority in his voice brought her back to the motel room, when he'd given her no choice but to obey him. If his intention was to push her away, his demands were having the opposite effect. Her pulse drummed loudly in her ears; her hands ached to run up his sculpted chest. She'd come out here to apologize for her lie, but now that they stood so close and she could feel the undeniable pull between them, she wondered if her lie had affected yesterday's outcome whatsoever. This attraction would have been there even if he'd known her identity from the beginning. She was sure of it. *This* wasn't a lie.

The girl she'd been before, the one who catapulted headlong into the unknown, wanted to push him to admit it. What they'd shared couldn't be chalked up to convenience. A way to kill time as the car was repaired. No, he'd shown her a part of himself she suspected he didn't reveal to many women. In turn, he'd taught her something about herself. Unlocked a side to her she hadn't known existed. Lucy closed the distance between them, letting her curves brush against him. His muscled chest heaved before her eyes. She could feel him, huge and straining at the front of his dress pants. For her. It was the final encouragement she needed. "I thought of you every time I sat down today. Just like you told me to,

Matt."

As if a rope had snapped inside him, Matt fell on her with a strangled groan. His hands dropped to her bottom, hauling her off the ground. Their mouths fought a battle, but she was too overcome with need to acknowledge the stakes. She processed movement, registered Matt walking them into a darkened doorway just off the street. Lucy tunneled her fingers through his hair, letting her head fall back as his teeth raked up the side of her neck.

"Goddammit, I shouldn't be doing this."

She gasped as he bit her ear. "W-what are you doing?"

"I'm considering giving you my cock right here and now. Would you like that, baby girl? Would you like to be rewarded for following my instructions?"

"Yes, please." She slid her inner thigh up his leg until it reached his waist, moaning when he gave a quick pump of his hips against her core. Already, she was damp for him. She felt trapped in between Matt's demanding body and the hard surface behind her. It was an amazing feeling. New and familiar at the same time, as though she'd been desperate to be immobilized without consciously knowing. When his hands wedged between their bodies to squeeze her breast with just the right amount of pressure, Lucy writhed, desperate for everything he could give her.

"What the fuck am I supposed to do, Lucy?" He grated the words against her lips. "Now that I've felt the tight squeeze between your legs? Watched your ass absorb my punishment? I'm fucked now, aren't I?"

"Matt," she breathed, trying to hook her legs more firmly around him. "I need to feel you again, too. Please."

A car passed, blaring music. She could feel Matt come back to himself then, as if an invisible tether had yanked him back to reality. His fist connected with the wall behind her as he slowly put distance between them. Lucy wanted to sob at the loss of pressure and heat.

"Come back," she said shakily.

"No. *No*," Matt ground out, frustration visible in the tight lines around his mouth. "Even if you weren't Brent's sister, which is more than enough in itself…"

"Yes?" Lucy prompted him after a moment.

Haunted eyes met hers. "I don't tolerate liars. Ever. I've been there. You're all the same and you never change."

Lucy couldn't move, couldn't breathe around the ache his words spawned in her chest. What could she say? He was right. She'd deceived him, making her the liar he accused her of being. Measuring her with a final look, Matt walked away and left her there, not glancing back once.

Chapter Seven

Matt stood in the precinct locker room, securing his Kevlar vest and buttoning his NYPD Emergency Service uniform shirt over it. When he heard Brent ribbing another officer in the next aisle, an uncomfortable feeling settled in his chest. He might have done the right thing by walking away from Lucy last night, but that hadn't stopped every imaginable sexual scenario from playing out in his head after he'd left. Starring Brent's deceptively sweet-looking little sister. Sure, she might taste sweet, but the things she'd said to him as they stood face-to-face on the sidewalk last night proved she was the furthest thing from it.

She'd known exactly what buttons to push to test his control. Looking up at him with those contrite green eyes, she'd stripped his defenses and tapped into his base desires so effortlessly it should have alarmed him. No one had ever seen through him like that. It was unacceptable. Only he'd been far from alarmed. He'd been turned on to the point of frenzy. Inside the party, his resolve had been unshakable. But with just the two of them standing there, memories sparking between them, everything had changed. She'd been asking him for something he desperately wanted to give her. What felt like his *duty* to give, even if that made no sense.

He'd gone home and unzipped his pants the second he walked in the door. Picturing Lucy's mouth, breasts, reddened ass, he'd pressed his forehead to the door and jacked himself off like a horny teenager. He'd thought one time would be enough. Then her words would drift through his head. *I thought of you every time I sat down today. Just like you told me to, Matt.* Just like that, he'd grow hard again, treating him to a vicious cycle that had lasted until the early hours of the morning. Still, *still*, he wasn't satisfied. Might never be again. Not after he'd experienced his real-life fantasies with Lucy. Making it twice as difficult, she wanted to do it again. Had begged him for more.

No. He couldn't allow it to happen. Not only did his desires have no place around a younger girl with a brighter future, but he hadn't lied to Lucy. Lying was a deal-breaker with him. For the first time, he welcomed a bitter memory that he normally kept hidden under lock and key, hoping it would serve as a distraction. His ex-fiancée's utter horror over his "disgusting" needs. Her seeking comfort from his best friend. It had all rushed to the surface last night when he found out Lucy lied to him. After exposing himself to her the way he'd done, it had felt like the worst kind of betrayal. It's why he was so careful about who he spent time with, who he could actually call a friend. Once you've been burned, that shit didn't come easy anymore.

Had the lie stopped him from wanting Lucy? Hell no. If anything, he wanted to find her this minute and punish her in a way that ended in her screaming his name. He wanted it so bad, his hands shook. The urge was painful to deny, especially knowing she would wrap that limber body around him and tell him to give it to her hard. *Fuck*. He had to stop thinking about her now or work would be impossible. Loss of focus in his line of work was tantamount to failure, and he refused to fail at his job.

Matt stowed his neatly folded street clothes in his locker just as Brent rounded the corner, followed by Daniel Chase, his other best friend. The newest member of their group, Troy Bennett, trailed behind, giving Matt a quick nod that he wordlessly returned. Matt had a hard enough time keeping two friends at a comfortable distance. He hadn't quite gotten around to figuring out how to fit Troy into his organized blueprint. Thankfully, Troy seemed just as content to maintain their casual acquaintance, not pushing for anything more.

He transferred his attention to Daniel, who had a look of exasperation on his face, which was usually the case any time he'd been talking to Brent.

When Brent caught sight of Matt, he did a double take. "Hey, dickhead. You just disappeared on us last night. You're lucky I don't have the ability to be insulted."

Daniel stripped off his shirt and threw it into his locker. "Yeah, you bailed before Story and I even got there. What gives?"

Matt started to answer with some vague excuse about being tired, but caught sight of the thin red scratch marks on Daniel's back first. Brent noticed at the same time and they exchanged a look. "What happened to your back, bro?

Daniel looked momentarily confused by the question, then he grinned. "Ah. It turns out my girl gets a little crazy after a few glasses of pink champagne. Didn't even make it in the door. Take note, gentlemen."

"Why, Daniel, you filthy animal."

Even though he felt like shit joking around with Brent after what had transpired with his sister, Matt couldn't help but be amused. "Maybe you should buy stock in the company."

Daniel pointed at him. "I like the way you think."

"All right, idea man. Enough stalling." Brent tugged his king-size Kevlar vest over his head. "Did you bail because of my sister, or what?"

Matt froze in the process of securing his locker. "Excuse me?"

"Lucy's accordion playing." Brent snickered. "She's been known to clear a room."

Actually, everything about her performance had been adorable. Her obvious nerves, the soft, husky quality of her voice as she sang in French. She'd practically sparkled. Such a parallel to his shadowed life, he could do nothing but stare, feeling ashamed of himself. He'd taken that girl, the blushing girl with curls framing her face, and used her to slake a need she had no business even being aware of. That thought had finally sent him out the door, needing to escape the reminder of what he'd done. How he wanted to do it again. And again.

Then she'd followed him and every self-issued warning had gone flying out the window in a matter of seconds.

Troy saved him from having to answer. "Why did you ask her to play if she's so terrible?"

"See, that's how this sibling thing works. I embarrass her because I love her." Brent strapped on his belt. "Don't worry, she's already thinking of a way to get me back. Let's just hope it doesn't involve burning my house down."

Or fucking your best friend blind. Feeling nauseous, Matt considered the possibility that Lucy might have seduced him to irritate her brother, but just as quickly, discarded the notion. She might have lied to him, but you couldn't fake their kind of chemistry. Or the way her body had responded under his treatment. *Christ. Stop thinking about her.*

Brent wasn't finished talking about his sister, however. "I should be getting a call any time now to come bail her out.

Maybe turn on the news and see her bungee jumping from the Chrysler Building."

Matt frowned into his locker. That didn't sound like the girl he'd spent the day with. A double major at Syracuse. Smart and logical, with an amazing sense of humor. A girl with job opportunities lined up. A detailed itinerary for her week in the city. *Then I heard you call me a nuisance…and I guess I just wanted to be someone who didn't inspire irritation. Just for one day.* Sympathy stirred inside him before he ground it to a halt. No way would he feel sympathy for her. Anger, yes. Lust, *hell* yes. But he wouldn't feel sorry for her. Not after she lied.

Daniel laughed. "She's still up to her old tricks?"

"Actually, she's been quiet lately. Must be gearing up for a big explosion." Brent slammed his locker shut and twisted the lock. "I haven't met her friend Sasha, who she brought with her from Syracuse, though. Maybe she's the good influence." He tipped his chin toward Matt. "You gave her a ride. What's she like, Matty?"

Matt's eyes slid shut and he fought the sudden urge to punch his locker. Lucy obviously hadn't told Brent she'd come alone. Why? He didn't know. Nor did he understand the wave of uneasiness that came with the knowledge that she'd be alone in the city all week. He only knew he was being dragged into her lie now. Making him something he hated. Unless he came clean now. Intending to do just that, he turned. Brent watched him expectantly, perpetually goofy smile in place. Matt couldn't do it. Maybe if he hadn't dragged her into a doorway last night and said all manner of dirty things to her, knowing full well who she was, he could have done it. But he had. He even wanted her again, despite her identity. And he didn't belong anywhere near her.

"Jesus, Matt. You were born in the wrong era." Brent finished tying the lace of his boot. "You would have made one hell of a silent film star."

All four of them received an emergency page at the same time. Matt breathed a sigh of relief as they holstered their weapons quickly and left the locker room. His mind should have been on the situation they were heading into.

Instead, he thought about the itinerary Lucy had accidentally left in his car.

• • •

Lucy picked a spot off to the side of the gathering crowd and spread her blanket down on the grass. She thought she'd gotten to Bryant Park early enough to get a better view, but it was fifteen minutes before the outdoor screening of *Back to the Future* was set to begin and the entire lawn was packed. Couples and groups of friends munched on popcorn or hot dogs; some moviegoers were even sneaking covert sips from brown paper bags. Evening had just fallen and the buzz of excited conversation made Lucy smile. She might be alone, but with so many people around, it didn't feel quite as lonely as she'd expected. The last six years of her life had been spent hunching over a textbook in a deathly silent library. There was no comparison.

She stretched her legs out on the blanket and kicked off her sandals, enjoying the warm breeze as it lifted the hair from her neck. It felt like she'd been living in jeans and a sweatshirt for most of grad school, so she'd worn a lightweight dress tonight. Freshly shaven legs, a sundress, and no assignments hanging over her head felt divine. She leaned back on her elbows and closed her eyes, for the first time letting herself enjoy what she'd accomplished. The feeling only lasted a few minutes because a prickling started along her scalp. Peeking one eye open, she moved into a cross-legged position and searched for the prickle source.

It didn't take her long at all to spot him. His stillness gave him away. Across the park, leaning against a tree with his arms crossed over his chest, stood Matt. For a split second, before he'd gotten his mask in place, she saw hunger tightening his darkly handsome features. It sent heat moving through Lucy in a slow ripple, making her aware of every inch of her exposed skin. She could hear the quick pace of her breathing, loud to her own ears. The blanket underneath her legs went from comfortable to caressing. What was he doing here? Did he come just to stand there in his uniform looking delicious, merely to torture her? If so, holy smokes, it was working. With desire coursing through her, she felt indecent just being in a public place with so many witnesses.

The movie started then, giant projection screen at the front of the park flashing white, then rolling the opening credits. Still, Matt didn't move. Why did it feel like he was touching her from a hundred yards away? Everyone around her had settled onto their blankets, wrapped up in nostalgia as Marty McFly enters Doc Brown's garage in the first scene. She tried to ignore Matt, she really did. He'd made it perfectly clear last night that he wanted nothing to do with her. But her gaze continually returned to him, making sure he was still there. His steady perusal of her distracted her to the point she couldn't focus on the movie. Finally, she'd had enough. She needed to force him into coming closer or leaving.

Please let him come closer.

Lucy unfolded her legs and slid forward onto her belly. She propped her chin on her hand, and crossing her ankles, she let her legs sway back and forth in the air behind her. It was a provocative pose, especially for a girl sitting by herself, but she took comfort in the fact that no one sat behind her to see her bare thighs on display. As she predicted, though, Matt didn't like it. When he pushed off the tree wearing a warning expression, a low thrumming began in Lucy's stomach, spreading lower with each passing second.

These instincts she had where Matt was concerned were completely new, yet she somehow trusted them. She knew what turned him on because it did the same to her. Driving him crazy, pushing his limits, made her feel desirable. It gave her a sense of control while simultaneously giving her permission to lose control. She wanted to tempt him past the point of return so he'd have no choice but to fulfill his needs with her. Somewhere underneath his stoic expression, he wanted it, too, or he wouldn't be here.

Hands clenching and unclenching at his sides, Lucy could tell he wanted to close the distance between them. She tossed her hair over her shoulder, exposing her neck, while at the same time writhing her hips ever-so-slightly on the blanket. When Matt began stalking his way to her through the crowd, she felt a surge of triumph, but lust quickly blanketed it. Female heads turned in his direction as he passed but he didn't remove his eyes from her once. Matt held an air of command at all times, but he wore his uniform today, only increasing his air of authority. She wanted to kiss him. She wanted him to refuse to kiss her. Nothing made sense any more.

Matt finally reached her, but she made no move to change her position. A growl lingering in his throat, he knelt down on the blanket beside her.

"Sit up," he commanded, keeping his voice low. "Immediately."

"I'm good."

His gaze lingered on her bottom before coasting down over her thighs. "You're the opposite of good."

Everything below her waist tightened. "W-what are you doing here?" she managed.

He sat back on the blanket keeping his legs bent, moving like such a sleek animal that Lucy's breathing faltered. "Your brother doesn't know you're alone. Apparently you weren't finished lying when I dropped you off on Friday."

His harsh comment hit home and she finally sat up, wondering if he'd known calling her on her lie would achieve his goal. "Mood killer," she muttered. "If you came here to knock me down another peg, it's not necessary. You did a bang-up job of it last night."

"I just came to check on you," he said curtly.

Anger sparked along her nerve endings. "I don't need to be checked on. I'm watching a movie in the park, not dancing topless in Times Square." When he only continued to watch her, she sighed. "Look, I didn't lie to him for the fun of it. He's got all this engagement stuff happening with Hayden. Not to mention the two jobs. I didn't want to be a—"

"Nuisance?"

Hearing him call her that—*again*—did not sit well. Lucy knew from experience that redness was climbing her neck, coloring her cheeks, and she refused to let him see it. She grabbed her purse and attempted to stand, but Matt curled an arm around her waist at the last second and dragged her down onto his lap.

"Hey. I didn't mean that." His voice rumbled at her neck and caused her to sag back against him, the new contact allowing his mouth to sift through the hair behind her ear. "Not the first time I said it. Not now. Okay?"

She blew out a breath. "Can you please strike it from your vocabulary, then?"

Matt hummed in his throat by way of answering. She couldn't help but marvel at how right it felt being held by him like this. Cradled against his chest, his body temperature warming every inch of her. Their bodies molded together, like they'd been superglued. How could she have missed touching him when they'd known each other such a short amount of time?

"What movie is this?" he asked into her hair.

Lucy's eyes shot wide. "*Back to the Future.* You've never seen it?"

"No."

"I weep for your childhood."

Matt's hesitant laughter rolled through her, but she quickly became distracted when his rough fingers began drawing patterns on her inner thigh, teasing the hem of her dress. He might as well have been stroking her between her legs for the sensations he was creating. "Catch me up."

"Huh?"

"On the movie. Tell me what's happening."

She tried to swallow but her mouth was dry. "Um… so. Doc Brown, the older gentleman who looks perpetually stressed out, has built a time machine."

"How?"

Lucy turned her head slightly and caught his clean leather scent. "Basically he souped up a DeLorean. And also…gigawatts."

"Gigawatts?"

"You kind of have to suspend your disbelief for this."

The corner of his mouth twitched. "Disbelief suspended."

Oh God, he really should smile more. "Marty goes back in time, but everything gets screwed up when his mother develops a crush on him."

"What kind of movie did you say this was?"

She laughed, but it emerged sounding breathless. "It's a classic." Matt's fingers inched higher on her leg, slipping underneath her dress, effectively cutting off her amusement. Her head fell back against his shoulder as he hooked his free arm around her midsection and positioned her higher on his lap. When his erection swelled underneath her bottom, Lucy released a shaky breath.

"Keep explaining. What happens to Marty?"

"You can't be serious."

"Me?" He tilted his hips once, twice. "I'm always serious."

"They go to the high school dance and Marty plays 'Johnny B. Goode' and happily ever after," she said all in one breath. With his big body surrounding her, arousal evident in his deep voice, yearning rolled through her, concentrated between her legs.

Matt took one corner of the blanket and tossed it over her lap. "Did you go to dances in high school, Lucy? Were you the bad girl who tempted all the boys? Yes, I think you were."

In one quick movement, he pushed aside her panties and shoved two thick fingers inside her. It took her by such surprise that a small scream would have escaped her throat if Matt hadn't covered her mouth and yanked her head back against his shoulder.

"Shh." His breath at her ear sent a delicious shiver down her spine. "Be very quiet and very still or everyone will know I'm fingering your pussy under this blanket. It needs to be our little secret, doesn't it, baby girl?"

When Lucy could breathe normally, she nodded. The illicitness of the situation hit her full force. Not only was this her brother's best friend, but he was an ESU officer. In uniform. She would have been lying to herself if she said the risk didn't crank up the yearning in her belly to overdrive. His fingers were high and tight inside her, creating heart-pounding pressure. It felt like her survival depended on what happened next. With a valiant effort, she tried to slow her shallow breathing and relax against him, so no one would notice what they were doing. Otherwise he might stop. *No. Don't stop.*

"Good girl, Lucy." His tongue outlined her ear, but still his fingers didn't move. "Your ass feels good sitting on my cock. We didn't get that far last time, did we?"

She whimpered into his hand, her hips beginning to circle of their own accord.

"If you don't stop that right now," he growled, "I'll take away my fingers. Do. Not. Move. You're going to sit like this the entire movie."

Immediately, her hips went still. She wanted to wail in frustration, but could do nothing but remain unmoving. His thumb brushed over her clitoris once, *only* once, and she started to shake. *Oh please, why won't he give me what I need? I need. I need.*

"You need to get off, Lucy? It wouldn't take much, maybe a couple strokes of my thumb and you'd get relief. I'd get to complete my shift with your pleasure on my fingers."

Lucy reached up and removed his hand from her mouth. "Please," she whispered. "Matt, I need it."

"Do you know how many times I came thinking about you last night?" He took a quick, angry bite of her shoulder. "Thinking about your hot, wet pussy?"

His words, the sting radiating from her shoulder, sent her closer to the precipice. All the while, the pressure grew and became more insistent, though he hadn't even moved his fingers. "I-I'm sorry. Please, Matt. It hurts."

"I thought you like the way I hurt you." His thumb jiggled her clit until her teeth bit so hard into her lip, she was sure she drew blood. Abruptly, he stopped. "Or was that a lie, too?"

Lucy's world tilted momentarily as his words registered. Her inner studio audience gasped in unison, one member of the front row fainting in shock. Is that why he'd come here? He was punishing her for lying? Even with a monsoon of hormones raging through her, the idea of him using her attraction against her was infuriating. Every moment they'd spent being physical had been honest. *This* moment was honest. She hadn't held a single part of herself back. Matt questioning her truthfulness when it came to the pleasure they'd experienced together…it felt like a betrayal. It made it, and *her*, feel cheap.

Lucy didn't know where she found the will to push his hand away and slide off his lap, but somehow she managed it. Matt tried to keep her against him, but released her when she started to struggle in earnest.

"Did you enjoy that?" she whispered furiously. "Torturing me?"

His expression was a mixture of confusion and stark arousal. "Lucy—"

"That was low, Matt." Her voice shook. "Getting back at me…like that."

If she hadn't been watching him closely, she would have missed the tinge of guilt that crossed his features. She'd been right. He *had* been punishing her. With no intention of giving her pleasure. He'd come here for some sick form of revenge.

"I'm not that hard up." She stood, backing away as Matt rose to his feet as well. "Don't come near me again."

Deciding to ditch the blanket instead of going anywhere near him, Lucy spun around and made for the street. She wasn't surprised to feel Matt's hand curl around her elbow before she reached the sidewalk. With a curse, he pulled her back against his chest. "You have the wrong idea. I didn't mean to—"

"If you're going to punish me, Matt…we both have to be on board for it. And I'm not. Not like that. I don't like feeling manipulated."

He pinched the bridge of his nose, opened his mouth to speak.

His two-way radio on his shoulder crackled to life. A nasally female voice released a series of codes that sounded foreign to her. One thing was obvious from his expression, though. He was needed somewhere else. Matt looked like he wanted to rip the thing off his body and hurl it into the nearest garbage can.

"We're going to talk about this," he said gruffly.

"What's the point?" Lucy pulled her purse higher on her shoulder and turned away. Her pride had been battered. Her body ached for something only Matt could give her. She needed to get away from him and think.

As she turned the corner toward Hayden's big, empty town house, there was an undeniable part of her begging him to follow, but she quashed it, increasing her pace instead.

Chapter Eight

Matt stood among the flashing blue and red lights on West Forty-Second Street as the final civilian was loaded into a waiting ambulance. A downtown city bus had overturned when the driver tried to take a left turn at too high a speed, crashing through a department store window. As a sniper, there hadn't been much for him to do in this situation besides assist rescue workers in carefully extricating the injured from the wrecked bus and blocking off the immediate area surrounding the accident. His particular skills were needed in vastly different situations, such as hostage standoffs or high-speed chases when a vehicle needed to be disabled from a distance. He spent the rest of his time on patrol, utilizing his other ESU training, as with tonight's situation.

Now that he had nothing left to distract him, his mind went immediately back to Lucy. With the thought of her came a wave of self-disgust so powerful, he wanted to break something with his bare hands. He'd severely fucked up tonight. Going to Bryant Park to check up on her, his intention had been to keep a safe distance, just to make sure no one bothered her. At least, that's what he'd told himself. If he was honest for two seconds, he would admit he'd been starving for the very sight of her. Then she'd been so close, lying in the grass, nighttime falling around her. She'd looked so damn beautiful in her dress, a content smile on her lips, he'd had no choice but to get closer. As if he'd been magnetized.

She hadn't been smiling for long, though. In typical Matt fashion, he'd found a way to ruin her night and break the trust she'd given him so freely. What he'd done to her in the park had been a form of torture, especially for a responsive, uninhibited girl like Lucy.

One look at her had rattled the chains he'd wrapped around his needs, tempting his inner demons to the surface. Demons that belonged in the past, but refused to stay there. He hadn't been able to get a handle on them or consider the consequences before he'd twisted her dishonesty into permission to punish her. By withholding her pleasure, he'd made her feel ashamed, or worse, ridiculed. Completely inexcusable. Lucy had nothing to do with his past or what it had done to him.

What she didn't realize is, demons or not, he wouldn't have been able to hold out much longer. He'd been desperate to feel her climax around his fingers.

Matt rubbed the back of his neck impatiently. The rational part of him insisted her outraged reaction was a good thing. In one fell swoop, he'd guaranteed she wouldn't come on to him ever again. She'd stop examining his body with those sea-glass eyes, as if she wanted to tear his clothes off at the first opportunity. Stop begging him with her body language for a repeat performance of their afternoon in the motel room. Hopefully, she'd decide she'd had enough fun dabbling in his world and move on.

Right?

Fuck no. Those were all mistruths he told himself in an

attempt to make them stick. To appease the conscience that told him over and over again, *you are not right for her. Or anyone.* He'd proven that tonight, hadn't he? Yet despite all that, what he really wanted, so badly his hands shook, was to go back in time and give her that orgasm. The kind that made her thighs clench and her words slur. The fact that he'd let her walk away unsatisfied made him feel like a caged animal. It might be fucked up, it might be completely off base, but he'd somehow taken mental responsibility for Lucy. Her pleasure. *Mine. I didn't satisfy what is mine.*

It was dangerous to think of her in those terms, because it could never happen. Look at how his control deserted him in her presence. He'd been down that road, watched people he'd known so well turn on him, look at him like a stranger. His messed-up past could never touch her. She saw him as one of her adventures and nothing else. While there was still time, he should walk away. Stop making excuses to see her. Touch her.

Instead, he found his ESU truck making the turn toward the Upper West Side, rather than downtown where he lived. The second he made the unconscious decision, he felt relief rush through him, which quickly became a low, steady simmering of heat underneath his skin. One more time. Just one more time so he could correct the error in judgment he'd made earlier. He wouldn't be able to sleep or eat or concentrate until he gave Lucy what he'd unwisely deprived her of underneath that blanket. His mind rebelled against any other outcome.

She needs me.

That thought overrode every warning in his head. *She's too clean. Too bright. You'll taint her. She's Brent's sister and you're seriously overstepping your bounds. Leave her alone.*

She needs me.

Fuck it, I need her, too.

Matt parked his vehicle outside the town house and took the steps two at a time. He paused briefly at the door, giving himself a moment to accept what going to her like this meant. It meant he wanted her despite the lie. It meant he would no longer have the right to hold it against her. It meant a giant *fuck you* to doing the right thing.

Already he was battling his body's demands and he couldn't think past them. For several long, anxious seconds, he didn't think she was going to answer the door, until he saw a shadow pass in front of the peephole. Then silence. She didn't want to open the door. His throat went tight over the realization.

"Let me in, Lucy." Jesus, he barely recognized his own voice. It sounded like he'd swallowed razor blades.

Nothing. She didn't respond and he heard no movement. He racked his brain, trying to remember some stray drop of knowledge he'd learned from Daniel's and Brent's headlong dives into couple-hood. *Anything* that could help him here. Then it came to him. Sorry. Men were always forgetting to just apologize. Hadn't *he* been the one to tell Brent that?

"I'm so damn sorry, baby." He sighed against the hard wood. "Open the door for me. I have to see you."

A lock turned and very slowly the door opened. Lucy stood before him in a white nightshirt that barely reached her thighs. Her eyes were puffy. From sleep or crying? His heart seized at the idea it could be the latter. Barefoot, hair tumbling around her cheeks, she looked so achingly fragile, he wanted to fall on his knees and bury his face against her skin. Absorb her warmth and give her his own in return.

"What are you doing here?" she asked, the wary note in her voice hitting him square in the stomach.

Matt didn't have the words. He rarely did. Everything had stayed locked up inside his head so long, he didn't know how to say the right thing anymore. So he braced his arm on the doorjamb and leaned in close, thanking God when her lips parted in awareness. He hadn't managed to obliterate her attraction to him, at least. "I'm sorry, Lucy." He took a chance and let his mouth graze hers gently. "I'm so sorry."

Her breath hitched as she swayed closer. "For what?"

"Not making you feel good when you needed it." He traced her lower lip with his tongue. "Let me in so I can fix it."

"Matt," she started, shaking her head. He was losing her, so he took it a step further. Couldn't afford to let her say no. He hooked one finger in the front of her low-rider panties and tugged her closer, satisfied when her eyelids drooped. "You probably shouldn't come in."

"No?" His hand coasted over her belly, then lower so his knuckle could run just under the edge of her underwear. "If you don't let me in, how am I going to find out if you're sweet all over?"

Seeing that he'd distracted her with that question, he backed her into the town house and kicked the door shut behind him.

"How do you intend to find that out?"

She knew. Matt could tell by the way her eyes challenged him from underneath her lashes. She just wanted to hear him say it. Christ, this girl made him hot. Somehow innocent, tempting, and challenging all at the same time. The wariness was still there, too, instilling a renewed urgency in him to replace the trepidation in her eyes with passion.

Her breasts were outlined by her thin T-shirt, alerting him to the fact that she didn't wear a bra. They rose and fell with her quickening breaths as she watched his face. A desire to get her out of that T-shirt so he could suck and lick his way over every inch of her gorgeous body burned everything else out of his universe. He realized his thoughts must be showing on his face because her own expression shifted, clouded with need.

Without wasting another moment, Matt brought his mouth down on hers. Goddamn. A groan ripped from his throat. He hadn't kissed her earlier and the feel of her lips brought on a fresh wave of heat. He'd forgotten what it felt like to slide his tongue along hers, feel her plump lips fall open to accommodate him. Kissing Lucy felt like breathing. He didn't have to think about it. They simply moved together, instinct taking over.

Reluctantly, he broke away to let her catch her breath. Already, his cock felt like it was being strangled in his pants. As she sucked in oxygen, he spoke against her lips.

"You going to give me a nice little taste, Lucy?"

Instead of answering, she threaded her fingers through his hair and tugged him down for another searing kiss. Matt cupped her bottom in his hands and boosted her up so she could wrap her legs around his waist. Immediately, she squeezed him and began a hot little writhing motion that had him stopping to press her up against the nearest wall, to give her three quick pumps of his hips.

"Hottest fuck of my life," he growled into her neck. "Can't think of a goddamn thing but getting back inside you. What did you do to me?"

No, he couldn't get lost in her like this. Tonight was about giving her what he'd deprived her of in the park. He couldn't *wait* to give it to her. With a growl, he yanked her off the wall and walked her into the living room. He broke their kiss to lay her on the nearest surface, an oversize ottoman in the opulent living room. God bless the girl, she tore her own shirt over her head, jostling her curls so they fell over one eye, making her look like a *Playboy* pinup instead of an accordion-playing grad student. She looked up at him, all swollen lips, upturned breasts, and excited green eyes, and his heart tripped all over itself.

If I'm not careful, she's going to rip me wide open.

When her fingers started working his belt buckle, he came back to himself. He took his shirt by the hem and discarded it on the floor. On hands and knees he prowled over her until she was forced onto her back, hands knocked loose from his belt. "No, no. I know you'd suck me so good. But my mouth will be giving the pleasure tonight."

He gave a long lick of her pert nipple and she moaned. "Twist my arm, why don't you?"

Matt trailed his tongue between her breasts, taking the other nipple between his lips and sucking, humming in his throat to send vibrations through her body. When her back arched, fingernails cutting into his shoulders, he trailed his touch up the inside of her thighs. They fell open for him, a show of submission that made him pulse with heat. With pride.

When he began to massage Lucy through her already-damp panties, she nearly came off the ottoman. "Matt. Oh my God."

"Did you touch yourself here when you got home, baby girl? Maybe watch a little porn to pick up where my fingers left off?"

She blushed, but shook her head frantically on the soft surface. "No."

Thank God. He'd wanted to be the one. "Tell me why."

"I don't know, I..." Her eyes squeezed shut. "I didn't want to give in to it. Didn't want to admit you got to me."

Would this girl ever stop surprising him? He shoved the material of her underwear aside and traced her seam with his middle finger. Damp. Beautiful. "But I do get to you. Don't I?"

"Yes," she whispered, slaying him. "I get to you, too."

He felt transparent in that moment, as though she could see right past his defenses. It alarmed him, forced him into

motion again before she could say something else and strip
him completely. Taking one final suck of her delicious breast,
he began dragging his tongue down her belly. It shuddered
underneath his treatment, her navel dipping in time with hot
little gasps. Without taking his lips from her warming skin, he
slid her panties down her legs, finally baring her completely.

"Look at you, spreading your legs for a kiss." He pushed
two fingers into her heat, swearing under his breath at the
slickness of her arousal. She threw her head back, hips lifting
and falling, just as uninhibited as he remembered. "The first
time I tongue you into coming, it's going to be an apology.
The second time will be a reward for waiting." He fell to his
knees and took his first intoxicating taste of Lucy. A growl
worked its way free of his chest. "The third time is going to
be because I fucking love to hear you scream."

"Matt. *Now*. Please!"

He wanted to take his time, but he couldn't stop once
he got started. The way she whimpered his name as his
tongue circled her clit made him feel like a god. In an effort
to get close as humanly possible, he threw her legs over his
shoulders and focused on turning her world upside down.
When her thighs began to clench and shake around his ears,
he drew his middle finger in and out of her entrance, sucking
with increasing pressure on that bundle of nerves that would
get her off. His cock was pressed against the ottoman, hips
pumping rhythmically as he imagined fucking her, being
surrounded by all that tight heat.

After a few too-brief moments, she dug her nails into his
hair and tugged, her flesh spasming against his mouth. "Oh
my God. It's so good. So good."

He continued his ministrations, but kept his eyes on her
bucking body as she came. Lucy getting off was the most
unbelievable sight he could remember. He'd feared her
becoming an addiction, and he saw now that his concern had

been more than warranted. His own condition was rapidly deteriorating, sending him into madness. Hunger pumped madly in his veins. He wouldn't give in to the impulse to climb on top of her body and ride her until he got tired of hearing his name screamed at the ceiling. As in, never. He wouldn't. This was for her. Only her.

When she settled down, Matt reached up with one hand and trailed his fingertips over her breast. "You are sweet all over, aren't you? Your mouth. Your nipples." Gently, he bit the inside of her thigh before licking away the sting. "Your pussy." His tongue found her center again, flicking her sensitive clitoris gently. "I like hearing you beg, baby. Do it again."

She moaned, taking her own hair in restless fists. "That was...I mean, holy—"

"Lucy." Matt pushed and dragged his painful erection against the side of the ottoman. "Again."

"No." She tried to sit up. "Come up here with me."

He pushed her thighs open with a growl. "*Yes. I'd like another one, please.* That's the correct response."

For one emotionally charged moment, she only watched him through hooded eyes, as if she might protest again. Until he savored her in a long, hard lick. Her body shuddered, knees falling wide once more. "Y-yes. I'd like another one, pleas— *Oh, God.*"

Chapter Nine

Lucy woke with a start when her internal studio audience began chanting her name, softly at first, then louder and louder. As if she'd done something to earn their approval. But what? Her eyes flew open, the events of the evening crashing through her memory like a rhinoceros in the jungle. Matt showing up at her door looking anguished. Hungry. Him pleasuring her from his knees her until her vocal cords went raw. He'd basically sent her into an orgasm coma. Should that fact cause her embarrassment or make her feel like a rock star?

Her studio audience immediately ceased chanting her name and started in with *rock star, rock star, rock star*! She felt her lips tilt up in a satisfied grin. Damn straight, rock star. Call her Mick Jagger because—

Someone shifted behind her in the gigantic guest bed and Lucy stifled a squeak of panic. A heavy arm slipped around her midsection, rugged male stubble scraping her neck, accompanied by a satisfied noise. A clean scent filled her nose, mouthwateringly masculine. It calmed her, even as it made her belly flutter with sudden nerves. Matt had *stayed over* last night? She didn't remember him carrying her to bed, nor had she let herself think past their stolen moments together. Not with Matt, who continued to be elusive.

Despite his attempt to punish her in the park, she'd quickly transitioned from anger to a puddle of trembling need. Something that seemed to happen frequently where Matt was concerned. She'd heard the rawness in his voice and had no choice but to open the door. His expression as he'd stood silhouetted by the streetlamp had been her final undoing. Regret had been a living thing written all over his face. Before she'd formed a rational thought, he'd been touching her, kissing her, talking to her in a hushed, overtly sexual manner that gave her goose bumps every time it whispered through her mind. Instead of giving him hell like she'd planned on doing if they ever crossed paths again, she'd spread her thighs quicker than a Pilates instructor.

She didn't know what it meant that he'd never, at any point last night, taken his own pleasure. She'd been more than willing to give it to him, remembered telling him so explicitly on more than one occasion, in fact. Yet he'd continued to deny himself, even though he'd been noticeably aroused. As in, wood for *days*. However, orgasms notwithstanding, they hadn't actually *talked* about what seemed to keep happening between them, so in the light of day, last night felt kind of like one of those dreams that leaves you feeling anxious and confused about its meaning.

His hips pushed against her bottom then, thoroughly distracting her. Arousal laced through her when she felt his erection, throbbing and insistent behind her. Since he hadn't spoken, she didn't know if he was awake or if his body did all the talking. His muscled arm tightened, drawing her back against his chest, grinding his hips slowly, melting her into a sensual puddle. She felt him shift, then the sound of a foil rapper being ripped open. His hand slipped between their bodies to roll on a condom.

"Going to fuck you now, Lucy," he growled into her hair.

Her breath caught. "About time."

His hand traced up her throat to her jaw and squeezed. "Watch the way you speak to me."

A furious beat began pounding within Lucy. How many sides were there to this man? Cherishing one minute, demanding the next. She couldn't keep up, yet both sides did incredible things to her. At the movie last night, she'd been upset over his using her lie as a reason to withhold pleasure, but up to that point the delayed gratification had been a huge turn-on. Even after what they'd done so far, she suspected he was still holding back. She wanted more…all of it.

"I'm sorry," she heard herself say, the sound of her hoarse apology somehow turning her on even more. So did the fact that she hadn't actually seen his face yet, only heard his voice, felt his body. It felt like an erotic fantasy, except her body's reactions told her she was most definitely wide-awake.

Swiftly, Matt yanked her panties down to her ankles. Holding her breath, she kicked them off the rest of the way, anxiously waiting for his next move. His hand rested on her knee for a moment, the touch in itself sending pings of electricity racing along her skin. Then he jerked it high and pulled it back to rest on his thigh, leaving her open, her center exposed.

"Did I, or did I not, lick your beautiful pussy last night until you lost consciousness?" He plunged two thick fingers inside her, making her moan loudly. "An answer, Lucy."

"Y-yes," she answered on a shudder. "That happened."

He rotated his fingers, leisurely stroking her sensitive inner walls. "So when you say 'about time' it makes me wonder what the hell you're talking about."

It didn't seem possible after the countless climaxes she'd reached last night, but her belly tightened again like a snare drum, an ache forming low and heavy, all controlled by Matt's hand. She racked her brain for a way to answer him that would make him continue touching her. "I was talking about you. You didn't—"

He delivered a sharp smack between her legs. "I didn't what?"

"*Ah!*" Shocked pleasure flooding her, Lucy searched for an adequate response. Her clitoris throbbed where he'd delivered the stinging slap. There was pain, but oh, mostly just driving need so strong she shook. "I wanted you inside me."

"Oh, I remember." His amused answer sent warm breath washing over her ear. "All your hot begging and moaning. *'Please, Matt. Fuck me. Fuck me. I need it so bad.'*" Another ringing slap between her thighs, right over her sensitive bundle of nerves. "Do you enjoy making me crazy?"

Lucy whimpered as his thumb stroked her clitoris. "A little bit, yeah."

"Wrong answer." Without warning, he drove his erection home inside of her. "*Fuuuuuck.*"

The same long, drawn-out blasphemy echoed in Lucy's head, but all that came out was a muffled scream. After hours of needing to be filled by Matt, it had finally happened and somehow it beat the memory of the last time, an incredible feat since he'd blown her mind in that motel room. He felt enormous, throbbing deep inside her, but he didn't move. She suspected he was calming himself, getting used to the sensation of their joined bodies. The evidence that she affected him as much as he affected her filled her with confidence. Made her feel wanted. Needed. Vital.

"Pull your knees up to your chest." His voice was gravel. "Keep them there. And hang the fuck on."

She drew her knees up and wrapped her arms beneath them, eyes fluttering closed in anticipation. When he mimicked her actions, overlapping her banded arms and pulling her tighter against him, they let out a simultaneous groan. She didn't think two people could get any closer than they were at that moment, her curled up on her side with his body enveloping her. "Oh, please. *Please*," she breathed, needing him to move.

Slowly, he withdrew, then rammed in deeper than before. "No more begging or you'll be doing it from your knees. Do you hear me?" He sounded as though he spoke through clenched teeth.

She nodded frantically. "Yes." *Again, again. Please keep moving.*

He took himself out inch by inch before driving back in, to the hilt. "I can still taste you on my tongue, baby. I woke up twice last night wanting more." Five quick thrusts had her sobbing his name. God, he went so deep. Deeper than she'd thought possible. "You trying to make me an addict?"

"Yes!" She shouted the word without thinking, but knew immediately it was true. Yes, right now, with him pinpointing every need in her trembling body with perfect precision, she wanted him addicted to her. She didn't care who knew or what he thought about it, either. Just needed more.

"Is that so?" His teeth bit into her shoulder, hips beginning to pump wildly. "Mission accomplished."

Her orgasm rose swiftly to the surface. Using what little leverage she had, Lucy worked her hips back and forth, meeting his thrusts. The friction sent her closer, so deliriously close, she could taste blood from where her teeth sank into her lips. A scream formed in her throat as it began to overtake her.

Matt slowed his assault, laughing darkly when she cried out. "You will wait, Lucy. I'm not ready to stop fucking you yet. And that's exactly what will happen if you tighten up on me. I'll blow straight into your pussy."

She felt dizzy and hot. Her legs were shaking out

of control, but she had no choice but to absorb his long, measured thrusts, even though she wanted to scream for him to go faster. "Oh God. I'm going to die."

Matt withdrew completely and flipped her onto her back. She had no time to prepare before he shoved her thighs wide and slammed into her. Over and over and over. He took her hands and pinned them over her head as he groaned into her neck. Lucy could only cry his name toward the ceiling as her release hovered close once more. She tried to hold back, knowing he would slow down if she showed signs of reaching the end. The sight of his sleek body and handsome, concentrated face above her wouldn't let her, though, and her core started to clench desperately around his arousal. She knew he felt it when he threw back his head on a moan.

"Matt, please. I can't *wait*."

Without pausing his brutal thrusts, he leaned down and bit her bottom lip. "You come because I allow it. You only do it for me."

"Yes. *Yes!*"

"Squeeze me, then. Milk it out of me."

Lucy raked her fingernails down his ass, yanking him closer as she contracted her inner walls. She kept her eyes open, memorizing the way his jaw went slack, eyes unseeing as he imploded, jerking heavily inside her. His potent reaction combined with the muscled flesh of his backside pumping beneath her palms sent her spiraling over the edge, her surroundings becoming insignificant as he worked her through a stunning orgasm.

"Goddammit, Lucy," he growled, collapsing on top of her. "I can't stop this. How can I stop?"

Her brain a pile of mush, Lucy could only thread her fingers through his hair, the action soothing them both. When he started to move off of her, she locked her legs around his hips to keep him there. He looked down at her for a quiet moment, then buried his face in her hair.

Shortly after, they fell back asleep.

• • •

Matt slowed his hurried gait as he walked into the kitchen and found Lucy perched on the counter, wearing an oversize Syracuse T-shirt. She didn't see him enter at first, looking deep in thought as she…roasted a marshmallow?

He shook his head and propped a shoulder against the wall to watch her, sure he was seeing things. She'd stretched out a wire coat hanger and impaled the fluffy white confection on the end, holding it over the gas burner. Beside her on the counter was an opened box of graham crackers and a king-size Hershey bar. She was making s'mores. At eight o'clock in the morning. The very idea seemed ridiculous, but when paired with Lucy, somehow it made perfect sense. Sunshine streamed in through the kitchen window, picking out the strawberry coloring of her hair, the entire scene a brutal reminder that she was everything he wasn't. A beacon of light while he stood across the room in the shadows. Everything inside him pushed him toward her, needing to touch that light, but he rebelled against it, convinced it might dim with his influence.

Minutes ago, when he'd woken up and found her gone, he'd been unreasonably panicked. They were in *her* bed, this is where she was *staying*. She couldn't have gone far. It hadn't stopped him from hurriedly dragging on his pants and striding out of the bedroom in pursuit of her.

Irrational. Everything about his reaction to this girl was irrational. He hadn't even meant to stay the night, merely wanted to hold her for a while. To know what it felt like. Next thing he'd known, he'd woken up and found her ass molded to his lap, his cock so hard he couldn't see reason or think straight. There had been no turning back at that point. *Get inside her or die.* The thought had rung in his skull, setting him on her like a starving man. He'd lacked control, dominating her, making demands...and loving the hell out of every single minute. Until he'd woken and found her gone.

He'd been too rough. Exposed too much of himself. She'd run.

He still didn't know if that was the case. She sat with her brow furrowed, rotating the marshmallow above the flame, a gentle hum emanating from her luscious lips, but she gave nothing away. Yet.

"S'mores aren't exactly a nutritious breakfast," Matt remarked, walking toward the refrigerator.

"*Oh!*" She jerked, knocking the box of graham crackers onto the ground. With a scowl, she shoved her curls behind her ears and slipped off the counter to retrieve it, careful to keep the marshmallow positioned correctly over the burner. As she bent over, he caught a glimpse of her pink boy shorts and barely restrained a growl. "Don't be grumpy. There's enough for both of us."

He raised an eyebrow. "I think I'll pass."

"Watching your figure?"

No, I'm watching yours. He cleared his throat and opened the refrigerator, seeing that it was empty save a carton of orange juice and green grapes. She'd gone to the store and bought the materials to make s'mores and nothing else? He sighed, shutting the fridge door. "All right. Make me one."

Her face lit up, cutting off the oxygen to his brain. "When Brent and I were kids—" She cut herself off, her pretty gaze flying to his when she realized she'd referred to the pink elephant in the room. Her brother. His best friend. Matt felt an uncomfortable churning in his gut but didn't say anything and after a moment, she notched her chin up and continued. "When we were kids, my mom refused to take us camping.

She hated bugs. *Anything* wildernessrelated, really. So once a year our dad moved the table out of the kitchen and pitched a tent. We made s'mores this way."

The way she smiled fondly at the memory made him want to dive across the kitchen and drag her into his arms, but once again, he stayed put. "Camping, Queens-style," he said, instead.

Her eyes twinkled. "Have you ever been camping?" When he only looked at her, she paled, obviously remembering the time he'd spent overseas living mostly outdoors. "Never mind. That was a stupid question."

Matt felt the insistent need to make her feel better. "Extreme camping, maybe. Minus the s'mores." He waited until she smiled again. The pressure in his chest eased. "We ate MREs. Field rations. Not as appetizing as what you're cooking, but they got the job done."

He watched as she very carefully placed a piece of chocolate on a graham cracker, then stacked a marshmallow and another graham cracker on top. Looking satisfied with herself, she handed the creation to him. When their fingers brushed, he felt it down to the soles of his feet. Judging from her intake of breath, she felt it, too. Her tongue danced along her lips. "What was your first meal when you came back?"

Such an odd question. Hell, this whole situation was odd. So why did he feel so at home? He bit into the s'more as he thought about her question, a grunt of approval escaping him before he could stop it. Damn, it tasted good. Not half as good as her, though. "A foot-long sub sandwich. Two, actually."

"Not something your mom made?" Oblivious to how her question threw him, she stuck another marshmallow onto the end of the wire. "I would ask for meat loaf and mashed potatoes. And several kinds of pie. Let's just say I'd be wearing sweatpants for a while."

He decided she could use some extra weight. Maybe then

he wouldn't feel so guilty about manhandling her. *Stop that line of thinking. You can't continue to have her. Leave her alone.* "My parents weren't there to cook for me when I got back, but the sub did the trick."

"Where were they?"

The s'more felt stuck in his throat. "My dad lost the use of his legs when I was young. They have a difficult time traveling." Matt didn't add that he hadn't seen his parents since before his deployment and only spoke with them on holidays. His father had long ago become his mother's full-time job, leaving very little time to travel. Or cook special meat loaf. Lucy didn't need to be dragged down with that knowledge, though, nor did he know how he'd react to her sympathy. He was very much afraid he would like it and take advantage. Bask in all that light as long as he could. Quickly, he diverted the attention from himself. "What's on your bucket list today?"

For long moments, she stared as if she wanted to question him further on his parents. He realized he was holding his breath, hoping for both of their sakes she'd let it drop. If she showed him an ounce of compassion, he'd be across the room buried in her before she could blink. He couldn't explain it. Only knew it would undo him, and he'd never shown that side of himself to another person. What lay on the other side of exposing himself like that?

"Are you sure you want to know?" she asked hesitantly.

Now he did. Was it dangerous? It better not be. "Tell me," he demanded.

She visibly shivered. Why? "Trapeze classes at Chelsea Pier." Her gaze flew to the clock. "Actually, I better go. One should not be late to defy death. It's bad luck."

He frowned when she jumped off the counter and started to leave the room. "Forgetting something?"

Her expression was puzzled. Until he turned off the

stove's burner with a flick of his wrist. Looking sheepish, she rubbed her bare foot against the opposite leg. "Don't tell Hayden?"

"I won't, if you promise not to break your neck today."

"I'll give it my best shot, coach."

"Jesus." He scrubbed a hand down his face. "Go get dressed. I'm coming with you."

Chapter Ten

Lucy stood with her arms raised as the trapeze instructor, Justin, harnessed her into the safety equipment. She actually worried for the poor guy's life more than her own, thanks to Matt standing ten feet away watching every movement through dangerously narrowed eyes. It was obvious that he didn't like the instructor having access to any part of her body, and based on Justin's strained expression, he'd picked up on Matt's not-so-subtle warning, too.

The trapeze school practiced outdoors during the summer, right on the Hudson River. A gentle summer breeze flitted across her skin, warm morning sun heating her neck and shoulders. It would be nice if *she* knew what the hell his possessive attitude meant. She'd been shocked when he offered to come with her today, but he'd just muttered something about it being his day off and having nothing else to do. Was he simply doing her brother a favor by looking out for her, or did he actually want to be here? Last night and this morning, he'd effectively scrambled her brain with extraordinary sex. Somewhere in Hayden's town house, her panties were still smoking. Talking to him in the kitchen afterward had felt...natural. Well, as natural as possible when a big man-panther who dripped sensuality stood bare-chested licking chocolate off his fingers. She'd been silently begging for him to lose the pants and commence round two, but she'd sensed him holding back.

Talk about confusing. Any other time, she would poke him in the chest and demand answers. It's how she operated. There was little sense in holding back and not speaking your mind. With Matt, however, she feared it would send him packing. It made her nervous. Set her off-balance. He sent mixed signals and she didn't know how to receive them. He'd told her he didn't tolerate liars, but he continued to show up, as if he couldn't stay away. She liked having him around, even if his intentions were far from clear, so she kept all her confusing thoughts to herself.

She tuned back in to Justin's safety spiel. "Your first jump, we'll keep it very simple. You'll swing back and forth a few times, just to get used to the bar. Then you'll release and fall into the net. Once you know the net is there and you've experienced it, you'll feel more confident about the next phase."

Matt crossed his arms. "Next phase?"

"I-if she's comfortable, we'll attempt a knee-hang."

Lucy did a little dance. "Swinging upside down? Boom, let's do it."

Justin nodded, shooting Matt an apprehensive look. "Only if you're comfortable."

Lucy didn't know if he was reassuring her or Matt, who looked two seconds from pulling out his badge and shutting the entire operation down.

"Okay, your belt is secure. Once we're on the platform, we'll attach it to the *very secure* safety lines." Justin looked as though he were embarking on a death march. "I'm going to take you up now."

"Cool—"

"Wait," Matt barked. Before she could decipher his intention, he strode toward them, looking incredibly determined. With one tug of her safety belt, she collided with his body and he was kissing her. Not a good-luck-I'll-catch-you-on-the-flip-side kiss. It was a brain-melting, I-will-make-you-very-sorry-if-you-get-hurt kiss that nearly buckled her knees and sent her crashing to the ground. His tongue swept in and claimed every corner of her mouth, his hand curling around her ponytail to tilt her head back in a gesture of ownership. She moaned into his mouth, surrendering to him on every level possible, but he pulled back all too soon, steadying her with a firm hand on her elbow.

"Wow," she breathed, immediately wanting to slap herself. Honestly, could she not take his lead and shroud herself in a little bit of mystery, too? Instead, she seemed bent on showing her hand at every opportunity. Perhaps that was the reason he showed up whenever he felt like it. She welcomed him with little urging on his part every time. The annoying realization caused her forehead to crease.

Matt frowned at her. "What's wrong?"

"I'm too easy."

"You're forcing me to watch while you put your life in the hands of a man wearing purple spandex." He shook his head. "You are anything but easy."

She felt her mouth stretch into a grin. "Thank you."

His jaw flexed as he moved closer, lowering his voice. "At the risk of distracting you, baby, you should know I'm dying to spank your ass right now until you scream."

Oh, holy hell. Her stomach felt like it had sprouted wings. "H-how is that not distracting?"

"I don't want you doing this."

She didn't hesitate. "Too bad. I'm doing it."

His eyes flared along with her already raging need. But she wouldn't give in. She'd already decided a moment ago that she'd done too much of that lately. Time to leave *him* wanting more for once. He obviously read the resolve in her eyes, because he huffed out a breath, giving one last tug of her belt to judge its secureness. "Go. I'll be right here."

"Good. I might need someone to catch me if I miss the net." She yelped as he made a grab for her, leaping out of his reach and jogging off to join a nervous-looking Justin. They climbed up the ladder to the platform, which Justin explained stood twenty-three feet high. When they reached the top, Lucy scanned her surroundings and took a deep, exhilarating breath. This is what she'd wanted after those grueling years of grad school. What she'd missed by buckling down and locking her wild side in a cage. She'd missed that feeling when you're about to embark on the unknown. Matt gave her that feeling, too. She just didn't know how long he'd stick around to give it to her.

No more icky thoughts. Focus on the positive.

Justin finished securing the safety lines to her belt, then handed her the trapeze bar. "Okay, now as I said, this first time is going to be really fun and easy. Just let yourself fly. Drop whenever you're ready and the net will catch you."

Lucy nodded once, squared her shoulders, and jumped.

. . .

Matt watched with a mixture of horror and awe as Lucy tucked her legs up to her chest and curled them around the bar. No. This was only her first jump, she wasn't supposed to go upside down this quickly. He hadn't been given enough time to mentally prepare for the sight of her dangling upside down like a monkey at the zoo, zipping through the air at a speed that made his heart seize. Oh, but she couldn't just dangle. Oh no. This crazy girl he couldn't get enough of had to fling her arms wide and arch her back, as if she'd been doing it her entire life.

Matt didn't even realize he'd started moving until he was positioned directly underneath her swinging form, watching her expression transform with absolute bliss. Her beauty and abandon sucked the air right out of his lungs. Yet at the same time, he was *jealous*. He wanted to be the only one who made her feel like that. If that wasn't a supremely dangerous and arrogant sentiment, he didn't know what was. That right didn't belong to him, nor did it have any place around her. It warned him that he needed to stay far, far away from her, even as he felt compelled to drag her off the trapeze and never let go. For the first time he could remember, he didn't know if the controlled part of him would win. Not where Lucy was concerned.

It terrified the ever-loving shit out of him.

She let go of the bar then. Time froze for Matt as she dropped, dropped...and landed. She bounced once into the air, letting out a delighted laugh that punctured his rib cage. He could only stand and watch as she rolled toward him and eased off the net to her feet. Their eyes locked and whatever she saw in his expression made the glow on her face dim. He hated that reaction, because he recognized it as inevitable. If he spent any length of time around her, he'd dim her until no more light existed. Knew it with absolute certainty.

Her hands began clawing at the safety wires, disconnecting them from her belt. "Is there a bathroom I can use?" she called to Purple Spandex.

"Inside the office, all the way in back. You don't want to do another jump first?" the asshole shouted back, making Matt want to strangle him.

"No. Not right now." She finally succeeded in freeing herself from the belt, dropping it to the ground and coming forward to take his hand. "Come on, Chuckles."

Matt followed her into the empty office, down the brightly lit hallway. He had no idea where they were going or what she wanted once they got there, only knew he couldn't turn down a chance to touch her. Not now, after he'd just watched her careen through the air and *let go*. Probably not ever. When she tried to pull him into the women's bathroom, he balked, but followed her in anyway.

When the door closed behind them, he heard someone breathing heavily and realized the sound came from him. A glance at his face in the mirror had him doing a double take. Jesus, he looked like shit. Worse, he felt shaky, anxious. Weighed down with need, not only of the sexual variety. Something more. Something urgent. He'd meant it earlier when he told her he wanted to spank her until she screamed. Watching her jump off the platform, then let go and free-fall, had left him feeling startlingly out of control. Control he needed to regain immediately.

Somehow, Lucy seemed to understand, coming to stand in front of him. "Whatever you need, take it."

He'd spun her around to face the sink before he'd commanded his hands to do so. He saw in the mirror the way she closed her eyes, mouth parting on a bracing inhale, and his cock swelled in his jeans. It made him want to hear her gasp his name. Sob it. Shout it. Made him desperate to hear the slap of her flesh. Without a trace of gentleness, he yanked down her black yoga pants and bared her tight, fuckable ass. "Brace your hands on the sink."

Reflected in the mirror, her breasts rose and fell temptingly. He reached around her with a rough hand and pulled down her neckline so he could watch them jiggle each time he slapped her. He found her nipples and pinched them roughly, her needy whimper making his vision blur.

"You drive me out of my goddamn mind, you know that?"

He ran his hand over her shoulder and down her back, ending at her upturned ass, kneading the flesh with his fingers. "You shouldn't want this. You shouldn't want my punishment. But you do, don't you? You're starved for it."

"I want it." She pushed back and twisted her hips. "Please."

A voice sped through his consciousness telling him this was wrong, that he was introducing her to something that she should never have to know about, but his body overruled the warning. Power licking through his veins, he leaned down and spoke very precisely near her ear. "I hope that motherfucker hears me spanking your ass until it's red. This first one is because I didn't like his hands on you. When it lands, I want to hear an apology."

He watched her eyes glaze over in the mirror, transforming her from the carefree girl flying through the air to someone else entirely. It shamed him. It made him hotter. Keeping their gazes locked, he brought his hand down with a loud *slap*. Her mouth opened on a silent scream, before she whispered something he couldn't hear.

"I didn't hear you, Lucy."

She pushed her ass into his hands, asking for more. "I'm sorry."

He couldn't stop from pressing her forward onto the sink, pumping his jeans-encased erection between her spread thighs at an erratic pace, until she cried out. Finally, he managed to drag himself away. "This next one is for being impulsive and not waiting for proper instruction before flipping upside down like a lunatic. You scared the hell out of me. An apology, Lucy."

His hand connecting with her flesh reverberated through the restroom, mingling with her throaty moan. If he checked, he knew she'd be wet and ready, but something wouldn't let him take her there, in the restroom. Did he actually have a shred of decency left? When she met his eyes and breathed her second apology, he stopped wondering and resolved to think about it later. At a time when he felt rational. He was getting there now, regaining his composure with every blow to her perfect backside. Every sound of pleasure coming from her lips. This sweet, carefree girl was curing him of his anxiety. And he was dragging her down into his pit.

Matt almost stopped then, the realization sobering him ever so slightly. Then she thrust her ass higher and bit that plump bottom lip, heavy-lidded gaze meeting his in the mirror. Her breasts were ripe, nipples pouting up at him. Christ, she was the most beautiful thing he'd ever seen. Too beautiful. Nothing could stop him from giving her that final blow. Verbally and physically.

He wrapped her ponytail in his fist and tilted her head back. "This last one is for letting me do this to you. For not running away every time you see me. Say you're sorry for letting me touch you."

Her eyes cleared, a hint of panic entering them. "No."

"Lucy," he grated. "You are not in control. You handed it to me when we walked in here."

"I don't care." Her voice shook. "I won't say it."

A frustrated growl ripped from his throat. He didn't know where he found the strength, but he released her, falling back against the bathroom door. She quickly tugged up her pants and turned to face him. He was horrified to see tears in her eyes.

"Why wouldn't you say it? Look at you." His voice sounded hollow, agonized. "Two days in a row I've made you cry. I bet you don't cry this much in a year."

She closed the distance between them and slipped her arms around his neck. He flinched at the contact because it felt so right. So damn right. He didn't deserve it after what he'd just done. How he'd ruined her morning with jealousy and control issues. "I lied to you once and I won't do it again. That's why I didn't say it." She pulled back and kissed his mouth lightly. "Drive me home?"

He closed his eyes so he couldn't see her. If he kept looking, he'd kiss her and lose himself. She'd make him forget about the shame and he wouldn't allow that. "You know I will."

They drove home in silence, although he could feel Lucy throwing occasional glances in his direction. He was glad she didn't speak or try to discuss what happened, how he'd overreacted. What the hell would he say? He had no explanation for what she did to him. Inside him. When they pulled up in front of the town house, he felt a flare of panic at the prospect of watching her leave, but reminded himself that her itinerary was at home on his kitchen table. He could relax marginally knowing where she'd be tomorrow, even if he knew he'd spend every moment until then convincing himself to stay away.

"Matt?"

Cautiously, he glanced at her. "Yeah."

"I would have made you meat loaf." Her hands fidgeted in her lap, but she held his stare. "For your first meal back, I mean. I would have made you meat loaf."

He couldn't summon words as she jumped out of the car and speed-walked toward the town house, dragging his bleeding heart along behind her.

Chapter Eleven

Lucy set her oversize tote bag down very gently in deference to its contents and plopped down beside it on the grass. Union Square Park was a beehive of activity even in the middle of a workday, couples sharing lunch from food trucks, dog walkers struggling to keep control of their charges, tourists mapping their next destination. She let her gaze wander over the interweaving crowd, looking for a sign of the group she'd come to meet. There were a few people meandering around on the steps, holding bags similar to hers. They made subtle eye contact with her, then looked away.

She hid her smile and leaned back in the grass, estimating she still had about five minutes before the event started. Five more minutes until she could effectively distract herself from memories of yesterday. She'd had very little luck in the distraction department last night and this morning. Considering she'd been pleasured within an inch of her life by an insanely gorgeous and complicated ESU officer, then spanked in a public restroom, she figured she got a pass.

Matt. What the hell was she going to do about him?

At the trapeze school yesterday, she'd glimpsed something inside him that should have scared her. Instead, she'd been drawn closer as if pulled by an invisible rope. To soothe, to reassure, in his own unique way. Perhaps it had been the promise of finally getting underneath his tough outer shell. Or maybe her attraction to him didn't allow for any other reaction apart from gravitating toward him. She hadn't liked seeing him that way, anxiety pouring off him in waves. Somehow, she'd done that to him, which had tripled her compulsion to make it better.

Say you're sorry for letting me touch you. She'd tossed and turned through the night trying to figure out what he'd meant by that. How could this gorgeous, larger-than-life man have a single insecurity? Yet that's exactly what she'd seen when he let down his emotional brick wall yesterday. The strong, confident man had been rendered momentarily vulnerable. But she'd been just as attracted to that part of him as she was to his dominant side. Didn't he realize that?

She groaned out loud at the memory of what she'd said to him as she exited the car. The feelings she'd revealed. *I would have made you meat loaf.* God, he likely thought she was either a simpleton or desperate. He must have broken the speed limit driving away from the town house. Combined with the scene in the bathroom, she probably wouldn't be seeing him again. The thought lodged in her throat, making it difficult to swallow.

When she experienced the distinct feeling of being watched, she rocketed back into a sitting position and looked around the park for the source. It wasn't just the feeling of being watched, it was the feeling of being *perused*. Studied. Heat traveled along her skin, beginning at her neck and moving down over her breasts and curling in her belly. She'd felt it at the outdoor movie, the same thickening of air around her. The sudden desire to be pushed down and ravaged. Matt was here. She just couldn't find him through the gathering crowd.

There. Leaning back against his ESU truck, about fifty yards away. Her mouth went dry at the sight of him looking so authoritative, eyes hidden behind a pair of Ray-Bans. Now she knew it wasn't just the uniform that made him seem so commanding. It was him. She knew the strict control he exercised and it excited the hell out of her. Even layered on top of the vulnerability she'd seen yesterday. Maybe more so because of it. God, she wanted him again. It startled her exactly how much.

At the moment, though, she'd settle for getting him to come over and simply talk to her. Then she remembered what was about to take place in the park. *Oh no,* he needed to stay put or he'd be in for a world of surprise and irritation. Quickly, she turned back around and pretended to be engrossed in her phone, hoping her lack of come-hitherness would keep him at a safe distance.

No luck. A moment later, a shadow darkened the ground around her. Dread in her stomach, she looked up and found Matt staring down at her, arms crossed over his chest. She couldn't deny that having him towering over her in his shit-stomping boots, badge clipped to his hip, made her hormones twirl around an imaginary stripper pole.

"Lucy."

His deep voice shivered its way through her. She could see herself reflected in his sunglasses, and her tiny likeness projected against his imposing figure made her dizzy. This man had brought her to the brink of insanity yesterday. How could he look so cool now? "How do you keep finding me?"

He glanced away. "You left your bucket list in my car."

Oh. "And that means you have to keep showing up?"

She had a feeling he was glowering at her behind those dark sunglasses. "If you would just tell Brent your friend canceled on you, that you're alone in the city all week, you wouldn't have to do everything on the list by yourself."

"Why haven't *you* told him?" When he didn't answer, she stood up and stepped into his personal space, looked up at him with all the seductiveness she could muster on short notice. "Maybe you like finding me alone, Chuckles?"

His jaw flexed, but still he said nothing.

Lucy sighed and stepped back. "He's all content in his domestic bliss. I didn't come here to throw a wrench into his engine, I came to help it run smoother."

Matt considered her for a long moment. "How do you plan to do that?"

"By getting a job, easing the pressure. Leaving him alone," she added under her breath.

He surprised her by laying a hand on her arm. "You really think you're doing him a favor, don't you?" When she simply looked at him, he shook his head. "You're wrong."

"Am I?" She glanced away. "You knew nothing about me the day we met. Nothing except what a shitload of trouble I am. A nuisance."

Matt's hand flew to her chin, tipping her face up. "If I ever hear of you calling yourself that again, I'm going to find you wherever you are and make you sorry."

Being this close to him, hearing the steel in his voice, tied her in knots. If given the opportunity, she might never get used to it. "Is that a promise?"

"That's a promise." Matt narrowed his eyes. "Anyway, you might be half a shitload of trouble, but definitely not a full one. Unless there is a trapeze involved."

"Think so?" She grinned. "I'm about to shoot that opinion to hell."

A whistle blew in the distance, telling her the event would begin in thirty seconds. She needed to warn Matt. He was already distracted, looking around them with a puzzled look on his face. Lucy turned to find that a huge crowd had gathered, all smiling in anticipation. "What is this, anyway? Your itinerary just said 'FM, Union Square.'"

Lucy bit her lip. "FM stands for flash mob."

"Jesus."

No sooner had the word left his mouth than a giant water balloon hit him square in the shoulder. Mouth open in shock, he looked at the wet spot on his uniform shirt, then down at Lucy. She couldn't help the laugh that bubbled in her throat. She clapped both hands over her mouth to keep it contained. "Oh, God. I think your uniform makes you a target."

The throngs of people behind her erupted in a series of battle cries as water balloons began flying, exploding on people and the pavement around them. Unsuspecting tourists scattered in every direction, some braver ones stopping to take pictures on their cell phone. She'd been right, though. Several participants were pointing at them, probably dying to get a shot at a member of law enforcement. She turned back to find Matt shaking his head.

"You better get out of here, Officer."

A water balloon narrowly missed his head. "Screw that. Where's your ammo?"

Lucy's eyebrows shot up, but she indicated the tote bag full of water balloons.

Matt reached down and grabbed the bag, taking her hand in the other. With a squeak of surprise, Lucy tripped behind him as he jogged to the nearest bench and pulled her down behind it. After yesterday, the last thing she'd expected to see was a playful side. Yet another facet of him, as if there weren't enough already. He set the bag between them, reached in and handed her a water balloon. "Let's see what you got, Mason."

A smile stretched across her face. "One point for every hipster you hit. Two for tourists."

His mouth twitched. "Done."

She peeked over the bench and hurled a pink balloon at a girl in horn-rimmed glasses. The unexpected impact of Lucy's balloon knocked them askew on her face.

"Nice one."

"One point for me." She tossed him a yellow balloon. "Your turn."

"Give me another one." With a shrug, she did as he asked. He pushed his sunglasses back on his head and Lucy suddenly wished she could drag her fingers through his thick black hair. In one fluid movement, he went up on his knees, throwing both balloons at once. Two running tourists were treated to an exploding water balloon attack.

"Impressive." Unable to wipe the grin off her face, she rooted through the bag. "It's like you're a professional sniper or something."

Matt's hand flexed, as if talking about his profession put the feel of a rifle in his hand. "Are you implying I have an unfair advantage?"

"I'm not implying. I'm accusing." She pulled out three balloons and threw him a wink. "Which means I have to step up my game."

His hot gaze raked over her. "You think you can compete with me?"

It was a wonder the balloons didn't turn to steam in her palms. "I never back down from a challenge, especially when the competition is meaningless and there are no prizes for winning. Watch and learn, Donovan."

He gestured arrogantly toward the quad area where the fight raged on. "I'm waiting."

Lucy peeked through the wooden slats in the bench, spotting a group of tourists wearing *I Love NY* T-shirts. They were a good distance away and had managed to remain dry thus far. It was a risk, but she'd talked a big game. *No guts no glory.* She pushed to her feet and threw all three balloons in quick succession, nailing each one of the tourists one after the other. Before they could spot her, she ducked back down behind the bench to find Matt staring at her with raised eyebrows.

"You are so turned on by me right now," she said, sounding a little breathless.

"Fucking right I am."

She had to kiss him. Had zero choice in the matter. His mouth, his *pleasure-giving* mouth, was gorgeous and so close. His body drew hers closer as if she'd become magnetized. She wanted his big, demanding hands on her ass. She wanted to feel his rough-edged muscles under her fingertips, flexing for her.

His teeth grazed his lower lip. "Come here then, baby."

Before she could reach him, a water balloon pegged him in the arm. He looked so disgusted over it, she had to laugh again. She planted her hands on his shoulders and tried her best to appear serious. "Oh God, Matt, you've been hit. Do *not* go toward the light. Stay with m—"

His mouth stamped over hers. As if he had complete and utter control over her body, she moaned, head tipping back to absorb every stroke of his tongue. She gloried in his uneven groans; they told her how much her submitting affected him. Told her there was a balance. That she shouldn't be afraid of her willingness to hand him the reins. It was a choice.

Matt felt it, too. Her total relinquishment of control. She could tell from his expression when he pulled back, scrutinizing her face. "You don't know what it means, Lucy."

"Tell me. Show me."

Lucy held her breath. She didn't know why his response was so important, only that it might make or break this thing between them. Once again, it became so obvious to her that there was so much about him she had yet to learn. She wanted to know everything. Anything less would seem like she was being cheated.

Expression regretful, he pushed her hair back, watching as her curls fell around her face. "Look at you. You live in the sun. I can't do it."

"Yes you can. You're here in the sun with me right now." The words came out in a rush. She barely knew what she was saying, only that she was losing him. The Matt who'd thrown water balloons was receding, to be replaced with the stoic, closed-off man he showed everyone else. "You just have to stay here with me."

"I wish it were that simple." He drew his hand back and Lucy bit back a denial. When the radio crackled on his shoulder, she slumped back. "I have to go."

Maybe adrenaline was still pumping through her veins from the water balloon flight or maybe their kiss had been a tease to her senses. It was even possible she didn't want him walking away without taking the best goddamn memory she could give him. Whatever the reason, she found herself lunging for Matt and kissing him for everything she was worth. Her fingers sank into his hair to keep him steady as she swept her tongue into his mouth. His growl of shock vibrated against her lips; his stubble scraped her chin.

He made a noise of capitulation and tried to deepen the kiss, but Lucy pulled away.

She looked him square in the eye. "Think about it. Think about me."

A humorless laugh escaped him. "You say that like it's optional."

Some inner voice urged her to her feet. She didn't want to watch him walk away, she *couldn't*, not after what he'd said. So she would leave first, even if it hurt to put distance in between them. "See you later, Matt."

She skirted past what was left of the balloon fight and descended into the nearest subway entrance, knowing instinctively he watched her the entire way.

Chapter Twelve

Matt sat at a red light in his ESU truck, performing the usual East Side patrol he'd been assigned to for the last six months. His fingers drummed on the steering wheel; a dull throb worked its way up the back of his neck. Every sound, every flash of sunlight off his windshield was an irritant. Even his jaw ached, he suspected from grinding his teeth together nonstop last night and this morning. Twenty-four hours without Lucy and he felt like a junkie who'd gone too long without a fix. How he'd already formed an addiction to the girl was beyond him. But he *had*. An all-consuming one that had stitched her beautiful image permanently on the inside of his eyelids. Caused him to catch her scent in the oddest places.

He couldn't focus on his job. Every thought led back to her, the way she'd looked yesterday. Full of life. Excitement. The way she'd made him feel it, too, during the brief, shining moment he'd *allowed* himself to feel. It had seemed too good to be true. He'd been forced to remind himself that he wasn't that man. The kind of man who made a girl like Lucy smile. He might be able to pull it off for one afternoon, but it couldn't last.

Tell me. Show me. She couldn't have known what those words meant when it came to him. They'd barely scratched the surface, even if the memory of his hand connecting with her flesh alone could bring him to his knees. When he allowed himself to fantasize about Lucy, he imagined her bound to his bed, under his command. He imagined her on her knees, wearing nothing but a chaste pair of white panties, waiting for his instructions.

The image caused an uncomfortable swelling between his legs and Matt couldn't resist granting his cock a tight stroke through his uniform pants. It only made matters worse, his thoughts escalating from Lucy on her knees to Lucy asking for permission to suck him off. His flesh disappearing for the first time past her pink lips.

Like this, Matt?

Teeth gritted in agony, he shook his head. Being an adventurous girl, she might be excited by the promise of a new experience, but was most likely just experimenting. Curious about the unknown. But for how long? What if his nature dimmed her free spirit before she'd had enough? He'd *never* forgive himself. At this point, he'd stopped warning himself off with the reminder of her family name. She was a Mason. Brent's little sister. If his best friend had an inkling of the thoughts plaguing him day and night, he'd have him in a pair of cement boots, sinking to the bottom of the Hudson. He'd deserve it, too.

Could she have meant it? Could she...accept me, just like this?

Another flashback projected itself in his mind, identical to the ones he'd been having all morning, whenever they'd managed to form a crack in his thoughts of Lucy. His ex-fiancée's expression of distaste when he finally revealed his needs. Her panicked look when she realized she'd agreed to marry a man with what she referred to as a "sickness."

Back then, he hadn't yet explored his urge to dominate in bed. It had been hiding somewhere in the back of his consciousness for as long as he could remember, but when he'd finally gotten the courage to admit what he needed, he'd been shut down cold. After that, he'd tried so hard to keep it under the surface, until he'd finally gotten the nerve to explore it one night, taking it just a little too far with someone who clearly didn't understand. He'd seen the emotional damage he could cause. The way she'd recoiled from him like he was a monster. That memory had been seared on his brain, only now it was Lucy's face, looking appalled, *repelled*, by what he kept tied up inside. Lucy turning to another man for comfort. A man with *normal* needs.

Matt pounded the steering wheel so hard it shook.

He wouldn't recover from that outcome. Not his time. Not with Lucy.

If he walked away now, it would be best for her. He knew that. It would ensure he didn't continue to disrespect his best friend by going behind his back, too. The fact that he'd let it go on this long was inexcusable. If he walked away now, Lucy would meet someone else. A man without a truckload of baggage and an ugly past. One who had the ability to treat her right. Brent would rib the poor guy constantly, but he'd be at peace with Lucy's choice in a way he would never be okay with Matt. His friend who'd taken advantage of his trust, pursuing his sister well past the point where he'd found out her identity.

Or he could take one more leap of faith. A shot in the dark that Lucy could allow him to explore his needs while he took unqualified care of hers. He could trust Lucy to know her own mind, giving him the chance to return the favor for the times she'd trusted him. He could...*show* her. Another surge of anticipation tore through him. To be with Lucy, guilt-free, no limits...

The light turned green. Instead of continuing down Second Avenue as his route dictated, Matt flipped a U-turn back toward the Upper East Side, where he knew Lucy and Brent were having lunch at Quincy's in half an hour.

• • •

Lucy sat on the steps of the Metropolitan Museum of Art sipping a Diet Coke through a straw and staring into space. Groups of students on field trips diverged around her, cabs honked, hot dog vendors yelled into their cell phones. The multitude of sounds swept along the warm summer breeze, barely registering. She hadn't exactly been in the best frame of mind for a job interview but thought it had gone surprisingly well. The young woman who'd interviewed her had been a Syracuse alum and they'd talked for an hour before actually getting down to business. If she was offered the job, she might even have a lunch buddy on day one. Luck seemed to be on her side.

At the very least, the interview had distracted her for an hour, and reminded her of her objective to become employed as soon as possible. Now however, against her admittedly weak will, her thoughts returned to Matt. He hadn't come to her last night. They'd made no plans to see each other. So why had she lain awake in bed, listening for the door? When it became obvious he wouldn't come, she'd tossed and turned in the enormous bed, her body feeling hot and achy. Throughout college and grad school, she'd rarely felt the compulsion to touch herself. She'd been exhausted from studying, too focused on other things. Yet last night, she'd found her hand slipping down the front of her panties before she'd made a conscious decision.

Lying facedown, she'd taken off her shirt so her nipples could rasp along the cool sheets. Her thighs had moved restlessly as she'd massaged herself in quick strokes, her moans muffled by the pillow. It had been taking too long— she'd been growing frustrated with the need for relief, her anger projected at Matt for not showing up. That's what had finally sent her flying. She'd thought of arguing with him, trying to walk away. Him stopping her. Holding her against the wall, demanding that she stop fighting him…before he'd resorted to touching her. Replacing her anger with reluctant pleasure. It hadn't been long before she submitted, in the fantasy and in reality. Before her climax had brought his name to her lips, over and over.

In the light of day, even she had to blush thinking about what her imagination had conjured up. His forcefulness in her fantasy had been the element that drove her to the brink. His refusal to relent. Matt's tastes seemed to be lighting a fire inside her, kindling wants she'd never known existed. She wanted to explore them, badly, but based on their final exchange yesterday and his absence last night, she had no idea where they stood.

He hadn't seemed comfortable sneaking around behind her brother's back, so why did he keep pursuing her? Did he desire her so much that he couldn't help it? A thrill moved through Lucy at the possibility that a man like Matt, usually in such ruthless control of his emotions, couldn't keep them in check around her. Still, she didn't like going behind Brent's back either. She'd been stupid and impulsive the first time, but the longer it went on, the guiltier she would be. In her eyes and Brent's.

If her brother ever found out. *If* there was something more than a physical attraction between her and Matt, he would have to be informed at some point. Otherwise, this would be chalked up to a forbidden affair with an end date, never to be acknowledged by anyone save her and Matt. The possibility of that outcome left her feeling more than a little empty.

She thought of her brother, of all he'd done for her. Helping raise her, paying for her college tuition, encouraging her in his own unique way. Her throat tightened with guilt. Next time she and Matt were alone, she would bite the bullet and ask him what he wanted to do. In the meantime, she had a lunch date with Brent at Quincy's on the East Side, meaning she needed to be across town in half an hour.

Standing to dust off the pencil skirt she'd worn for the interview, Lucy prayed it wouldn't be too difficult to look him in the eye.

Right on time, she walked into the buzzing pub and immediately spotted her brother sitting at a table near the back. Not that he was difficult to spot since his size made him a foot taller than most people in the establishment. Since today happened to be his day off, he wore a pair of old faded jean and a Mets T-shirt. When he saw her, he broke into a smile.

"Look at you, dressed to kill." He kissed her on the cheek, then gave her a look of alarm. "Hold up. You didn't actually kill anyone, right?"

With a smirk, she hung her purse on the back of the chair. "Job interview. Idiot."

Brent shrugged as he sat back down. "The day is young."

"Keep it up and you'll be my first victim."

As Lucy got settled in her chair, Brent signaled the waitress. "Job interviews already, huh? You finished grad school all of four days ago."

She accepted a menu from the waitress. "The sooner the better."

Her brother watched her closely. "Yeah? Why is that?" He leaned back in his chair. "I thought you'd be itching to backpack around Europe or join the circus."

I want to help you. I don't want to be a burden anymore. I want to be a solution, not a problem. "The circus isn't hiring at the moment."

"All the bearded lady positions have been filled?"

Their banter felt so comfortable and familiar, she had to bury her smile behind her menu. "Something like that." Deciding on the turkey club—she *always* got the turkey club—she tossed the menu onto the table. "Funny you should mention Europe, though, I had an offer—"

"*Matty,*" Brent shouted over her shoulder, making her jump. With a pit in the bottom of her stomach, Lucy turned and saw Matt standing just inside the door, wearing his ESU uniform. Every pulse point skittered at the sight of him. When their gazes met, every inch of skin covered by her clothes flamed. She thought she saw his eyes flare with want, just as she imagined her own doing, but he turned and gave the waitress his order before she could be certain. As he approached them, she tried to read his expression. This had to be awkward for him. But she couldn't gauge anything from his expression.

"Figured I'd grab some lunch to go," Matt said by way of greeting. "I'm on duty for another four hours."

"Sit with us while you wait, bro." Brent kicked out a chair beside her. "Lucy was just telling me about her job interview today."

Matt glanced at her, mask perfectly in place. "Really. Where?"

She suddenly hated that mask. Wanted to shout at him until it went away. "The Met."

"The *Met*?" Brent slapped the table. "Are you kidding me, Luce? Why didn't you say something?"

"I kind of just did." She shifted in her seat, trying to ignore the heat radiating from Matt's thigh. "Anyway, it's just an assistant position. I'd be working under one of the curators. Probably doing Starbucks runs until I get blisters."

In reality, it was a coveted position for someone fresh out of grad school. She'd been persistent about getting the interview, even having a handful of her more connected professors write letters of recommendation. It would put her right where she needed to move higher up the ladder, giving her valuable experience in the process. If she ever decided to move on, her résumé would be rock solid, having worked at the world-famous museum. Should they decide she was right for the position after today's interview, she would accept the job in a heartbeat. It meant living her dream *and* being close to her family.

The waitress dropped off drinks Brent had ordered, effectively distracting her brother with a cheap shot about the Mets. Lucy glanced up to find Matt considering her closely. There was something behind his eyes that hadn't been there a moment ago, as if he were working on making a decision. His gray stare was serious as usual, but something *else* existed behind it. Hope?

When he reached under the table and took her hand, she had to work hard to keep her features schooled. He laid his other hand on the table, giving her the impression he was bracing himself. The hope she thought she'd seen morphed into determination, and she *knew.*

Oh my God, he's going to tell my brother about us.

Equal parts warmth and anxiety expanded inside her, encompassing every inch. This man she'd become fascinated with, the man she desperately wanted the chance to know better, was holding her hand, mere inches from her brother. He had to feel the same way, if he was risking his friendship with Brent like this.

Matt took a deep breath and turned to her brother. "Brent, there's something—"

"Hold up." Her brother set his fresh beer down on the

table with a *thunk*. "Before you came in, Lucy was about to say something. About another offer."

Every breath she took felt like it was being sucked in through a straw, to the point it took her a moment to catch up. What had her brother asked her? *Another job offer. Right.*

With a concerted effort, Lucy gave her brother her attention. "Y-yes. I was offered a job at the Louvre. In Paris. As a research assistant to one of the acquisition directors."

"Paris?" Brent looked simultaneously elated and crestfallen. "That's…great." He ran a hand through is dark blond hair. "Also, holy shit, that's far."

Matt's hand went cold in hers. She wanted to gauge his expression, but couldn't while Brent watched her so closely. "Yes, it's far, but—"

"Does it pay more than the Met position?"

She thought back to the e-mails she'd exchanged with the director. "Yes," she had to admit. "Quite a bit more, actually. And it includes housing, but I haven't—"

"Wow." He shook his head. "I can't say I'm happy about you moving so far away, but I could never hold you back, Luce. It's a great opportunity."

Lucy scowled at him. Rationally, she knew her brother was only being supportive, but mostly she just heard him sending her packing across the Atlantic without asking what she wanted, or even attempting to keep her close. It hurt like hell.

Matt nodded once, his jaw flexing. "That's great, Lucy. Looks like all that hard work paid off. You should take the offer."

His words fell heavily on her ears. The determination in his face was gone. In fact, his eyes held no trace of emotion at all. Had she misjudged his intention to reveal their relationship to Brent?

Feeling as though someone were stepping on her lungs,

she released his hand under the table. No sense in pretending to be anything more than a casual hookup. Even if she hadn't misjudged, if he was willing to let their chance to be together fizzle and die without a fight, maybe it was a good thing he hadn't come clean. She wanted a man who *would* fight for her, damn the consequences.

"Well, this blows." Brent let out a breath and nodded at Matt. "What were you going to say, anyway?"

Briefly, Matt's gaze flashed to Lucy. "Nothing. Except, your car has a ticket on it. You forgot to put your NYPD registration in the window again."

"*Dammit.*"

Lucy didn't turn around as Matt turned and strode from Quincy's. But before he even reached the door, she'd shed her devastation...and gotten good and pissed.

Chapter Thirteen

Matt knew the second Lucy sensed his presence. Across the street, her lips parted slightly on a deep breath, shoulders tightening almost imperceptibly. The fact that she didn't turn her head to seek him out told him she'd known he would come. It also meant she'd decided to be finished with him. He didn't blame her, even as everything inside him powerfully, *hatefully*, rebelled at that assumption. Furthermore, he should *not* be here. He'd fucked his chances yesterday. Damning himself with his silence in Quincy's. Clearly his actions, or lack thereof, hadn't been lost on her.

When he thought of the hope he'd seen in her eyes after he'd taken her hand…it made him feel sick with guilt. Livid with himself for not being the steadfast man she deserved.

He'd walked into the restaurant with every intention of revealing his feelings in front of her brother. Not spending every night of the foreseeable future with her tucked against his chest had been a hell he didn't want to face. His vision of walking out of there holding her hand, whether or not he had two black eyes, was mere moments from being a reality.

Then…Paris.

She'd told him about the job offer on the drive from Syracuse, but that day she'd been Sasha. Not Lucy. He'd chalked it up to a fabrication. Obviously, it hadn't been. He'd already been less-than-confident about his ability to make her happy. Even now, she stood among a group of strangers, preparing to salsa dance. In public. All by herself. She was brave and spirited. He would dim that part of her in no time. He'd seen ugly things, continued to see them every day. Hell, his job was to take people out when no other option existed. He couldn't compete with the possibilities she had laid out in front of her.

He'd been willing to try. To take a leap of faith because the way he felt about her left him no choice. But he wouldn't be the reason she turned down such an amazing opportunity. He'd asked a woman to put her life on hold once before while he fought overseas. She'd grown bitter and resentful. Unfaithful. She'd ended up hating him. That is exactly what would happen if he pursued Lucy. The pain from that would go *far* beyond what his ex-fiancée had been capable of inflicting.

So what the hell was he doing here? He should by lying low, letting her move on and get ready for Paris. Only, her left-behind itinerary had taunted him from his kitchen table. *Sunset Salsa 6:00, Lincoln Center.* He'd tried to stay away. He *really* had. But the thought of letting her fly thousands of miles away without an explanation didn't work for him. He needed her to understand why he'd backed off when he'd really wanted to drag her onto his lap and beg her to stay in New York.

Matt had come for another reason, though. One that pumped in his blood and refused to listen to rational thought. The idea of Lucy dancing outdoors, around other males… basically, that didn't fucking fly with him. No matter how many times he told himself it was none of his business.

What the hell are you going to do about it? You don't dance. She won't even look at you.

He'd lose his goddamn mind. That's what he would do.

She swayed to the Latin music, watching closely as the instructor explained the basic moves. In a red sundress that outlined her breasts, belly, and hips, hair swept off her neck in a clip, she looked like a delicious piece of forbidden fruit.

Matt wanted to devour her in one bite.

It was more than that, though. Her look of concentration, the way she moved her mouth as if repeating the instructor's words under her breath...he could watch her all day and never tire of it. She made him want to fuck. To lay his head in her lap and listen to her talk. To shake her until she admitted it would never work between them.

Yet *forbidden* was the only way to describe her. Forbidden to *him*. Not the endless stream of men who would flock to her positive energy wherever she went. Until she picked one of the bastards and decided to give him her trust, her body. Her smile. The very idea of it made him want to repeatedly slam his head against the steering wheel of his car.

He should leave. *Now.* Just put the car in drive and pull away. Too bad he couldn't even fool himself into thinking that was a possibility. He'd come here knowing exactly what would happen. Any second now, some asshole would try to dance with her and he'd be there to stop it. Didn't have a choice in the matter. Maybe when she moved across the Atlantic, he'd be able to deal with the idea of her with someone else. Someone who wasn't him.

Not likely.

Until she left New York, however, the possessiveness she'd coaxed to life inside of him had started making the decisions. The drumming in his chest that insisted she was *his* steadily picked up its pace. A muscle ticked in his jaw, counting the seconds.

Then it happened. Dancers began to pair off. He saw two men converge on her at once and didn't wait to see any more. He threw the car in drive and entered an underground pay parking structure located on the adjacent side street. After parking in the first available spot, which much to his frustration ended up being all the way in back, he exited the vehicle at a fast clip. When the attendant came forward to take his keys, he flashed his badge and kept walking. The halogen lights above him gave off an electrical buzz, matching the one sounding in his head.

His pace didn't slow as he rounded the corner and the quad filled with dancers came into view. He saw Lucy immediately, standing out as she did in her red dress. She threw her head back, laughing at something the man in front of her said. The man who was standing far too close.

The man who was at least ninety.

Matt stopped at the edge of the quad. When Lucy looked over at him sharply, he realized he'd been laughing. That brought him up short. He couldn't remember the last time he'd laughed so loud. So freely. It felt unnatural. It felt... really good. His feet started moving before he'd made a conscious decision, only knowing he needed to be near her. She watched him approach warily, appearing to do her best to pay attention to her partner.

The closer he got, the louder his heart pounded. "Lucy." God, it felt good just to say her name out loud. Some of the pressure drained from his chest.

She raised a single eyebrow. "Yes?"

"Can we talk?"

"Not right now." She nodded at her partner. "I'm dancing with Maurice."

Maurice saluted him. "Is she yours?"

Yes. The answer boomed inside his head, but didn't

translate to his lips. He didn't know how Lucy would react. Furthermore, he knew if he said it out loud, it would be so. There would be no going back, and she couldn't be his.

That momentary hesitation caused Lucy's cheeks to flush red. "Go away, Matt."

Maurice shook his head, then turned to Lucy. "I have a grandson. He's a musician, though," he added in a warning tone.

"Does he dance?"

"Honey, that's *all* he does."

She shot a pointed look at Matt. "Sold."

A couple dancing behind him nearly plowed into him, so he stepped closer to Lucy. "I understand why you're upset, but what happened…it was for the best."

• • •

The studio audience inside Lucy's head erupted in a series of boos and hisses. Even the host shook his head sadly, letting the microphone drop to his thigh.

She had the sudden urge to take off her high heels and hurl them at Matt, screaming obscenities and cursing him to a lifetime of blue balls. Instead, she kept her smile firmly in place and did her honest best to ignore him. Not an easy accomplishment when he stood there looking so *climbable*. Where did he get off filling out a black T-shirt and jeans like that? As if a tailor had sewn them onto him, leaving just the right amount of room to accommodate the cut muscles of his arms, chest, and legs, even better than his uniform normally did. She had a sudden memory of running her hands up those sculpted pecs, how they'd flexed beneath her fingers. How much he'd liked it.

Maurice. Focus on Maurice. Don't think about the way Matt is looking at you. That mixture of lost and hungry. It did funny things to her senses.

Yesterday, while she'd been silently willing him to grab on to her with both hands and never let go, he'd balked, trampling all over her feelings like a stampeding herd of buffalo. Holding her hand one second, sending her packing the next. If he'd come here to offer her some consolation prize in the form of half-assed explanations, he could keep them. She wasn't interested.

The alternative, that he'd come here for sex, was painful to consider. But maybe her assumption that they were more had been just that. An assumption. What other conclusion could she draw when he touched her at every available opportunity, but refused to say the words?

A part of her, the destructive side she'd worked so hard to tame over the years, wanted to take this game he was playing with her heart and flip it on its arrogant head. Would it make her feel better to give him a taste of that bitter medicine? Perhaps not. But at this point, she couldn't think of any other option apart from listening to his explanation, and caving in to whatever he asked of her, be it a strictly physical relationship or understanding. She didn't want to understand. Didn't have the capacity for it at the moment when her heart felt so damn heavy.

She could, however, take charge of the situation and end this game between them on her own terms. One last time to feed the attraction. She could handle that. One last time to show him what he'd be missing when *she* voluntarily walked away, with her pride intact.

Lucy ignored the little voice in her head that told her it was a bad idea. She'd once been an expert at ignoring that voice and tapped into that girl now. Being someone else for the moment helped mask the hurt.

The song ended and she stepped back from Maurice, whose eyes shifted between her and Matt with interest. Matt still stood there watching her, like an immovable brick wall. "You still want to have that talk?"

Surprise crossed his features before he hid it. "Yes. I would."

She nodded, then turned back to Maurice, kissing him on both cheeks. "It has been a distinct pleasure, my dear."

"You come back next week." He patted her shoulder. "I'll bring my grandson."

"She won't be here next week," Matt said.

"I won't? Why is that?"

He frowned. "You're going to Paris."

"I am?" She skirted past him, doing her best to hide the satisfaction rippling through her. "That's news to me."

A second later, he caught up with her. Her heart clenched a little when he took her hand, but it was only to lead her in the opposite direction. "My car is in the garage. We'll go somewhere and *talk*." A beat passed. "You're going to Paris."

Lucy blinked away the stupid moisture that sprung to her eyes. "God, one minute you won't leave me alone, the next you can't wait to get rid of me. I hereby declare you the champion of mixed signals."

"Why would you pass that up?"

She didn't answer his question. They entered the garage and she was grateful for the dimness. She needed to be cool, in control, and she couldn't do that if her eyes were shining. She knew he was waiting for her to answer his question as they walked deeper into the underground parking structure, but she refused. His car came into sight and an alarm signal went off in her head. She couldn't get into that car with him. If they went somewhere, if they talked, it would be harder to walk away from him afterward. As she'd known he would, he walked to the passenger side to open the door for her.

Before he could reach it, she let her body slide against his, biting her lip to keep from moaning. Why did his body have to hit her in all the right spots? Taking a deep breath, she gave in to her earlier fantasy of running his hands over his chest. "Why don't you stop pretending you want to talk?"

His eyes were dark, throat working as she touched him, but her words made him do a double take. "What does that mean?"

Lucy lightly dragged her nails down his chest and abdomen, watching him shudder. When her hands started working his belt buckle, he groaned and fit their mouths together. He pulled back after only one kiss, even though she could tell it cost him. "What are you doing, baby? This isn't why I came to get you."

She unzipped his jeans and reached inside to stroke his heavy erection. "Liar."

Matt braced his hands on the roof of his car. "Fuck. You're going to have to stop this. I don't know how to stop when it comes to you."

"I don't want to stop."

Chapter Fourteen

"Ah, God." Matt's eyes squeezed shut. "Please. I can do better than a parking garage."

The raw agony in his voice, his words, heightened her own need, even as they brought on a surge of affection that had no place here. She wanted to push him past his breaking point. Couldn't wait to see it. Her thumb brushed over the head of his arousal.

"Maybe you're scared to find out how deep I can take your—"

"*Enough.*" With a growl, he opened the back door and pushed her down onto the seat. Rough hands yanked down the top of her dress, exposing her breasts. His cheeks were flushed red, teeth scraping over his bottom lip. He looked torn for only a moment before he slapped one of her breasts, just enough to sting, enough to draw a whimper from her throat. His fingers gripped her chin and tipped it up. "You'll watch your mouth when you speak to me."

"Yes, Matt." When he released her chin, she leaned forward and ran her tongue up the underside of his erection.

His knees bumped the seat as he moaned. "Do you like that?"

"Fuck yes, I like it." He encircled the base of his arousal in one hand, guiding it to her already-parting mouth. "More. Now."

It had been a while since Lucy did this and never with a man Matt's size. She forced herself to relax and focus on what his body told her. What he responded to. Soon, she became lost in her own enjoyment. His taste. The strangled sounds she ripped from his throat. The way her scalp tingled as he pulled her hair, gently moving her fast, then slow, then fast again.

"You like the way I taste, baby?" His hips rocked forward. "No, you goddamn love it."

Lucy hummed in her throat, locking her fingers around his girth, stroking him off in time with her mouth. She heard his breathing begin to grow choppy. The fingers in her hair grew punishing, telling he was close to reaching his peak. He tried to draw her away with frantic hands, but Lucy didn't want to stop.

"You want me to finish in your disrespectful little mouth? You want to make my fucking life?"

Slowly, she nodded, relaxing her throat to let him slide deep, deeper than before, purring in order to send vibrations coursing through his hard flesh. Her mouth traveled up and down, increasing in pace, dragging her teeth lightly up the sides when he begged her to slow down. He was right at the edge. She wanted to see him come apart, was dying to witness it, but he dragged her mouth away at the last second.

"Next time," he barked, digging a condom from his jeans pocket and rolling it down his straining erection. "Spread your legs. Let me see the part of you that squeezes me so tight."

Lucy drew up her knees, letting her dress drift down to her waist. Her bare breasts were heaving; her lips felt heavy and swollen. Matt's hot gaze between her legs made her squirm on the seat impatiently. "Hurry," she whispered shakily, when he started stroking himself.

Matt grabbed her ankles and propped them on opposite ends of the doorframe, her high heels somehow still on her feet. He maintained eye contact with her as he ripped her panties off with a twist of his wrist, then leaned down to lick along her center. Two long strokes of his tongue that made her thighs begin to tremble uncontrollably.

"No screaming," he rasped. She hadn't quite processed his warning before he dragged the head of his arousal through her folds, then plowed deep into her. Lucy bit her lip hard, muffling the scream that ripped from deep inside her chest. The sound ended in a sob when he didn't immediately move. She needed him to thrust, but he stayed still, so deep inside her she could feel him pulsing. "I swear to Christ, baby, you were made for me. You feel that?" He pulled out of her, then slammed home once more. "*Mine. My* Lucy. Let me hear you say it."

No. She couldn't give in to his words, even though she desperately wanted to repeat them back. They felt true, but she knew they weren't. Her body might succumb to him, but her mind couldn't. Even now, her lower stomach muscles were coiled tightly, preparing for the inevitable rush only Matt could provide. She struggled to hold back, wanting to tug him down for a kiss but biting her lip instead. After this, she would walk away. This couldn't be about affection.

Matt must have sensed the tension in her because his eyes narrowed on her face. "You don't get to hold back. Not when I'm ten inches deep, Lucy. I won't allow it."

She rolled her hips on the seat, felt a spark of satisfaction when his breath shook. "You're the one holding back. Don't you want to move inside me, Matt?"

His hands flexed on her thighs. "Not until you're here

with me. *Say it.*"

Why was he doing this? What did he *want* from her? "No."

The strain was beginning to get to him. His ridged abdomen dipped and shuddered, his voice sounding unnatural. It wouldn't take much to tempt him into forgetting whatever mission he was suddenly on. Lucy trailed her hand up her stomach, brushing her fingers over her nipples.

With a strangled sound, Matt grabbed her wrists and tried to pin them behind her back, but she struggled to get them free. "Stop it," she said, but the words ended on a gasp. The friction caused by her struggle sent shock waves through her body. Automatically, her legs wrapped around his waist, high heels digging into his ass.

"*My* Lucy."

"*No.*"

"Your body disagrees," he growled, pushing deep as a means of pinning her. "You want the hard fuck I've got saved up for you? Say the words."

She hated him in that moment, even as she craved his body, the feel of him inside her, more than the air in her lungs. There were so many layers to this sensation of being restrained. The way he accomplished it with his powerful body, refusing to budge. His rejection yesterday opposing his wanting to claim her today. None of it made sense.

"What do you *want* from me, Matt?"

"I tried to tell myself wanting you, keeping you, was selfish. Maybe it is." His lips brushed her forehead. "But I'm lost here, Lucy. I'm lost without everything you've got."

It hurt. Not voicing the words of love threatening to burst forth, keeping them trapped inside, even as being held immobile by him made her body sing. Emotions, chaotic and contradictory, built in her chest until she could no longer contain it.

"I'm giving you what I have left, Matt," she sobbed. "Take it."

"You have more. Give it to me."

Acting on its own, her hand reared back and slapped him hard across the face. For a brief moment, the only sound was their labored breathing, before Matt sprang into motion, finally succeeding in pinning her hands over her head on the leather seat. The now-familiar excitement gathered in Lucy's middle and spread to every corner of her body, her mind.

Matt watched her closely, conflict in every plane of his face, his thick flesh still throbbing inside her. When he finally spoke, his voice was pure gravel. "Stop here or keep fucking you? I need an answer. And I need it *now*."

She squeezed him with her inner walls before allowing her thighs to fall open in invitation. At the same time, she struggled to get her hands free. "Don't give me a choice."

"Lucy...," he warned, even as his eyes darkened, then closed.

Refusing to give up on the feeling she was chasing, Lucy turned her head and sank her teeth into his forearm. The hands manacling her own tightened their punishing grip as Matt groaned. Lucy increased her struggle, bucking her body beneath his once, twice.

Slowly, his hips eased back, then pushed forward again. Euphoria shot straight through her body. She tossed her head back on the seat, reveling in it for a glorious moment, then began her renewed struggles. As she watched, Matt lost whatever battle he'd been waging inside himself and began to drive into her. When Lucy twisted on the seat, in a halfhearted attempt to dislodge him, he only threw her legs over his broad shoulders and pumped harder.

"Don't you dare try to keep that pussy away from me. It's mine. *You* are mine."

Somehow Lucy managed to speak around the pleasure

spearing through her. Oh God, she was so close. Just a little more. "No."

With a frustrated sound, Matt brought his body down on top of hers, bringing her knees even with her shoulders. Angling his body above her, he pounded down, grunting with exertion. "Give it up, baby. I feel you shaking for me."

She tossed her head on the seat, but couldn't vocalize her denial. He looked so male, so dominant above her, demanding a release she didn't want to give, but couldn't refuse herself.

Matt kissed her hard, thrusting his tongue deep. "I remember what it feels like when you're getting ready to blow. It's seared on my fucking brain. Any minute now, you're going to tighten up on me like a vise." He nipped her bottom lip. "And I'm going to fuck right through it."

Lucy didn't sail or drift over the edge, but catapulted headlong into a black chasm. She vaguely registered Matt's hand covering her mouth as she shouted his name, but pleasure overrode any other thought. Her body, already hot, reached a boiling point as she climaxed. It wouldn't end either, continuing to pummel her senses as Matt drove into her again and again.

Finally, he buried his face in her neck and let go, moaning scattered words against her fevered skin. "Sexy girl, my girl. Please. Baby, baby, baby. So good. So tight."

Matt released her hands and they went to his hair, sinking into the thick strands, stroking his scalp. Unconsciously offering comfort and praise. His weight on top of her felt unbelievable, as did clean the scent of his shampoo. She wanted to stay like that forever, unconventional a setting as it was. A sense of contentment tingled along her spine.

That's when Lucy knew she had to get the hell out of there. As she lay there, cradling Matt to her chest, holding him as his body vibrated in the aftermath of their lovemaking, it became brutally obvious she had serious, incurable feelings for him. She'd been stupid to think she could give him a mind-blowing sexual experience and walk away whistling Dixie, secure in her retained pride. With every encounter, sexual or otherwise, this connection she felt between them grew. Once again, she'd been too impulsive and it would cost her now.

But she had to go. Continuing like this, maintaining a physical relationship behind closed doors, would kill her. She inhaled deeply of his scent one final time, then wiggled underneath Matt until he stood back outside the car. Penetrating her with his eyes, he helped her sit up and fix her dress with gentle hands, so different from how they'd been minutes before. She did her best to keep her gaze averted as she searched the car for her purse.

"Lucy. Look at me."

Allowing a smile to form, she kept the rest of her face blank. As in, *would you like fries with that?* "I have to go."

His eyebrows shot up. "The fuck you do. Not like this."

A hot clench in her belly had Lucy grinding her teeth. That forcefulness in Matt could be her downfall if she wasn't careful. "I have a job interview." Another lie. Might as well swing for the fences.

"At seven o'clock at night?"

She shrugged and tried to hop off the seat. "Is this the city that never sleeps, or isn't it?"

Matt blocked her. "Why are you still interviewing?" His voice thickened with some unnamed emotion. "You're taking the Paris job. You told me on the drive from Syracuse that you loved it there."

Oh, that did it. She couldn't remain cool one second longer. With both hands, she shoved against his chest. He barely moved, inciting her wrath even further. "I'm *not* taking the Paris job, you moron. But don't worry, my staying in New York has nothing to do with you. I know the score. So don't worry about me. I know what this is." She skirted past him.

"It's *nothing*."

"Bullshit, it's nothing." He planted a hand on her shoulder, but she shrugged it off. "I haven't stopped thinking about you since the coffee shop. You never *leave* me."

Dammit. Tears gathered in her eyes. "I'm leaving you now."

"No," he breathed.

"*Yes*. You can't just show up whenever you feel like screwing me, Matt. I'm better than that."

Her words brought him up short. "Jesus, Lucy. I'm sorry I made you feel that way." He fell back against his car. "You're better than *me*. That's what this is about."

Lucy's anger took a nosedive. "Explain that to me."

"You actually have to ask me after I fuck you in a parking garage?" His throat worked as he glanced toward the opposite end of the underground space. After a stretch of silence, he pushed off the car and closed the distance between them. Lucy couldn't breathe, the look in his eyes was so fierce. "Listen to me, I—"

Sirens. The loud, continuous sound drowned out whatever Matt was going to say. It didn't stop, but continued to grow louder, the sound of speeding police vehicles above their heads impossible to ignore. Lucy and Matt exchanged a glance that she didn't need words to interpret. She nodded once and he strode back to his car, pulling his cell phone from the console. As she watched him closely, his muscles went rigid under his T-shirt, right hand flexing at his side in a familiar gesture. She remembered seeing it when he spoke about being a sniper. A feeling of dread settled in the pit of her stomach.

"What's wrong?"

When his gaze met hers, it was perfectly blank. That alarmed her even more. "Everything will be fine, but I'm needed downtown."

Lucy forced her lips to move. "It sounds like everyone is."

"Get in the car. I'll drop you off on the way."

She waved him off. "I'll be okay. Hayden's place isn't far from here."

"I'm not leaving you here." His voice was deathly silent. "If I don't get you home, I won't be able to concentrate. Get in, please."

She didn't ask why he needed his full concentration, just moved as quickly as she could toward the passenger side and climbed inside. He peeled out of the parking spot and had her in front of Hayden's town house within minutes. She tried not to let panic set in as sirens flew past them on every single avenue. Lucy wanted to ask what was happening, if he would be all right, but was terrified of the answer. Minutes ago, she'd been prepared to walk away from him, but in light of the danger she sensed, the very idea seemed absurd. She wanted to throw her arms around him and beg him to stay. His stiff posture forbade it, though. Wherever he was headed when he left her, it had his full attention.

As she climbed out, she looked back. "Be careful, Matt."

After a single nod, he pulled away, leaving Lucy staring after him on the sidewalk.

Chapter Fifteen

Matt lay perfectly still on his stomach, watching the building across the street, his finger resting on the trigger of his rifle. He could see the man in his scope, could take him down with a single shot. If he didn't have a bomb strapped to his chest capable of decimating an entire city block, he would have already done it. Instead, he'd been ordered to hold his fire and wait. His perch in the tenth-floor window of a high-rise gave Matt an unobstructed view into the bank where the man paced back and forth. The NYPD had evacuated the bank building as much as possible, through side exits and back doors, in addition to the surrounding area. However, the customers on the main floor of the bank stood huddled together, looks of horror on their faces as the man continually ignored phone calls from Daniel, who had been called to the scene as lead hostage negotiator.

In his ear piece, Matt could hear his friend's low curse as his call into the bank's main line went unanswered for the fourth time. Daniel, along with Brent, their explosives expert, and dozens of ESU officers were on the first floor, ten stories beneath him. With such vastly different specialties, the three of them were rarely called in at the same time, but this situation required each of their specific talents. Especially Brent's, although Matt prayed like hell he didn't have to walk into that bank. *Please don't let it come to that.*

Back at the parking garage, he'd seen the emergency message on his department cell phone calling him to a scene involving highly volatile explosives. He hadn't been able to tell Lucy. To look her in the face after already hurting her once and explain what kind of situation he and Brent were heading into. If she'd shown an ounce of worry or fear, he would never have been able to drive away.

As usual when he was in this position, the noise around him faded into nothingness, his measured breaths coming in time with his heartbeat. The drumming in his chest felt different this time, though. Not as steady as usual. Duller. More than a little painful as it knocked rhythmically against his rib cage. The silence he'd created around him couldn't stop Lucy's words from drifting through his head. *I know the score. I know what this is. It's nothing.*

He swallowed around the knot in his throat and tried to push the words to the back of his head, where he *would* deal with them later, but they stubbornly refused to fade. She refused to fade. Her injured expression. The lack of sparkle in her eyes. He'd done that to her, goddammit. All along, he'd known it was inevitable, but seeing it had been devastating.

What the hell had he been thinking? She'd slid her hot curves over his body, looked up at him as if to say *I need it good and hard, Matt*, and he'd lost his battle with common sense. He'd been incapable of stopping himself from drilling her against that seat, even as the voice inside his head warned him something was off. Her demeanor, her distant attitude… her Lucy-ness had been missing. At first. She hadn't been able to hold back once he pushed inside of her. What happened after that... Sweet Jesus. They way she'd writhed on his cock, thighs wide open for him as she'd pushed against him with her hands. *Bit* him. The contradiction of her resistance and capitulation had been mind-blowingly hot. Toward the end, he'd been heedless to anything but his body's demands, completely consumed by her. Again that voice in his head had implored him to slow it down, kiss her, look her in the eye until he got Lucy back, but there had been no stopping at that point.

Then before he could blink, it had been too late. She'd been walking away, such finality in her tone that he'd been frozen in denial. If she could walk away after what they'd just shared, he'd done some serious damage, but he had no experience repairing his own destruction. Only causing it. He only hoped it wasn't too late to fix it. No, he wouldn't *let* it be too late. There was way too much at stake this time.

Focus. You have a job to do first.

Matt breathed deeply through his nose and focused on the target, who looked completely calm, resigned. Oddly enough, that wasn't unusual for a man in his situation. He'd had time to come to terms with what he was attempting to do. While he was overseas, Matt had seen more than his share of this type of event, but it was rare to say the least in New York City.

Matt frowned. Also rare? The amount of time it was taking the man to detonate the bomb. If he wouldn't open a line of communication with Daniel to state his demands, what was his goal? At this point, he would only succeed in bringing a handful of civilians with him.

Then it happened. If Matt had blinked, he would have missed it. Subtly, the man checked his watch and glanced through the window at the building across the street. The building he and hundreds of ESU officers were stationed inside. Matt's heart began pounding loudly in his ears as he reached for the radio on his shoulder.

"Evacuate the building now. Get everyone out."

Immediately, his chief's harried voice responded. "Donovan? Wh—"

"He's a decoy. Move everyone out. Now." His own voice sounded distant. "We're the target."

Matt didn't bother waiting for an order. He shouldered his rifle and moved at a fast clip toward the stairs. Before he'd made it halfway to the lobby, the ground began to shake under his feet.

• • •

Lucy hadn't made it a full minute before turning on Hayden's massive flat screen and flipping to the local news station. What she saw had made her heart stop.

Suicide Bomber Holds Bank Customers Hostage.

She hadn't been able to fathom it. A bomb. That meant... her brother and Matt were *both* there? Smack in the middle of harm's way. After having held Matt in her arms only minutes before, it had been surreal. And terrifying. His stoic expression after he'd been called to the scene came back to her, suddenly making far too much sense. From there, it had only gotten worse.

Explosion Rocks Lower Manhattan. Number of Casualties Unknown.

She had no idea how long she stood there, still as death, in front of the television, worst-case scenarios materializing in her head before she could stop them. Her brother...Matt... she replayed every minute she'd spent with them over the last few days until she realized tears were coursing down her cheeks.

A commercial break for toothpaste had finally snapped her out of her stupor. As soon as she'd lowered herself onto the couch, her cell phone started to ring. She'd fumbled to answer it, praying it was her brother. Matt didn't even have her phone number. How ridiculous was that?

It had been Hayden calling.

"I'm home. I haven't heard from Brent yet. Can you... come over and sit with me?"

Lucy had found herself in a cab, heading toward Queens, before she was even aware her feet were moving. Home. That was where she wanted to be. Not some giant, unfamiliar house in a neighborhood where nobody knew her name. Her soon-to-be sister-in-law had to be worried sick, much like herself. Twenty minutes later, she walked into the front door of her childhood home. The differences were startling since the last time she'd been there.

Accent walls? *Sconces?* When had that happened?

Hayden appeared in front of her, wringing her hands. "Brent redecorated. He said he wanted to chick-ify it for me." She looked shell-shocked. "I'm marrying a man who dismantles bombs for a living. Am I a fucking lunatic or what?"

They both laughed, but it died just as quickly.

Lucy set her purse down. "Do you have anything to drink?"

"Tequila in the cabinet."

She nodded and went to the kitchen. "Are you partaking?"

In an absent motion, Hayden smoothed a hand over her belly, but Lucy caught it. "No, I'm fine for now. You drink mine."

Lucy swallowed the lump in her throat. She poured half a shot's worth into a coffee mug, then changed her mind and poured another two fingers. When she walked into the living room, Hayden stood in front of the television, watching footage of the explosion being filmed by a circling helicopter. She looked so ready to buckle from tension that Lucy knew she needed a distraction. Hell, she desperately needed one herself.

"How are the wedding plans coming?"

Hayden looked at her blankly. "What?"

"If I know my brother, he probably wants a Mets theme. Blue and orange all the way. Hot dogs and beer at the reception…" Lucy took a bracing sip. "Instead of a priest, you can have an announcer pronounce you man and wife through a loudspeaker. Then Brent can throw out the first pitch."

Hayden burst into tears.

"Shit." She set down her mug of tequila and led Hayden toward the couch. "He's going to be fine. Have you seen the guy? If a meteor fell out of the sky, it would bounce right off him."

That got a watery laugh. "He didn't eat breakfast this morning. I don't know why that bothers me so much. Maybe because I'm the one who distracted him." She swiped at her eyes. "He must have been starving right before it happened. That's all I keep thinking."

Lucy understood more than she knew. The scene with Matt played itself out in her head nonstop, ending the same way each time. His whispered denial when she tried to leave, that now-familiar haunted expression she still didn't fully understand. Had she put him off his game, right before he headed into a dangerous situation? The possibility continued to gnaw at her gut until she couldn't sit still any longer.

"Why don't we go make Brent something to eat, so it's ready when he gets here?"

Hayden nodded purposefully. "Yes."

"What's he eating these days?"

"What's he *not* eating?"

They worked for a while in the kitchen until Lucy gently suggested an exhausted-looking Hayden go lie down. To Lucy's surprise, she hadn't protested, sweeping from the kitchen without another word. Lucy wandered back out to the living room, muting the television before it drove her insane. The silence and lack of distraction were a bad idea, because she had more time to think about Matt. Earlier today, she'd realized her feelings for him ran deeper than she'd expected. She hadn't known the half. Losing him before she had that chance to peel away his layers. Oh God, if something happened to him...

A car pulled up in the driveway. Before she even knew her feet were moving, Lucy had flung the door open. Brent. He stood in the driveway looking weary and covered in filth, two butterfly bandages over his right eye and a white wrap circling his left forearm. Relief poured over her head like a bucket of sand that his injuries weren't worse.

He dragged a bag of gear from the back seat and shut the door. "Hey, Luce."

She swallowed hard. "Something wrong with your phone?"

"Actually, yeah. It exploded."

"Oh." She sniffed. "I hate it when that happens."

Brent smirked, but his expression turned serious. "Could have been a lot worse. If we'd been inside a few seconds longer, they'd be fitting me for size extra-large wings about now." He rubbed his forehead. "Only a handful of men injured, none dead."

The pressure returned to her chest. "How did you get out in time?"

He sighed. "Let's just say Matt picked a good time to start speaking up."

"So he's...okay?"

"Yeah. He was in the stairwell at the time...the safest place he could have been. Lucky fucker escaped with a couple of cuts." Her brother glanced at her funny. Before he could say more, his eyes caught on something behind her.

Or someone, rather. Lucy turned to find Hayden standing in the doorframe, wearing nothing but one of Brent's king-size T-shirts that ended below her knees. Her eyes were red-rimmed and puffy.

"Duchess, what did we say about going pants-less in public?"

"I'm wearing shorts."

"Now there's a shame."

"I'm pregnant."

Brent dropped his bag on the driveway. "What?"

"I'm pregnant and you almost got blown up, you ass," Hayden said shakily. "I'm never speaking to you again."

He went toward her slowly, laying a reverent hand on her belly. "There could be a mini-duchess in here?" His exhale sounded shaky. "Holy shit."

Lucy shifted beside them, feeling like an interloper. This was a private moment and she didn't belong there. She was starting to wonder if she belonged anywhere. Quietly, she slipped into the house to retrieve her purse, intending to take the train back to Manhattan. As she turned to leave, Brent walked through the door, carrying Hayden in his arms.

"Are you taking prenatal vitamins?"

"That's your first question?"

"It got you talking to me, didn't it?"

Hayden halted their progress by patting Brent on the shoulder. "Lucy, don't go."

"You heard the woman, I almost got blown up. That calls for a beer." He drew Hayden a little closer. "Not for you. You get water."

Lucy shook her head, suddenly choking with the need to get out of there. It didn't matter that she loved her brother and suspected Hayden would eventually be one of her favorite people in the world, she didn't want to be there. Seeing them so happily wrapped up in each other…it was somehow painful when it should fill her with joy. She knew the reason, too, making it even worse. She shouldn't be craving the same thing with Matt. Not when he didn't want it with her. But she couldn't help wishing he would look at her the way Brent looked at Hayden. With so much love it could barely be contained.

"I have to go." She forced a smile onto her face. "I'm really glad you didn't explode."

He didn't laugh as she expected. Instead, both of them were watching her with concern. She couldn't get to the door fast enough. No way would she spoil their moment with her own problems. With a wave, she slipped out of the house and into the evening.

The subway ride back to Manhattan seemed to pass in the blink of an eye, the car rattling around her, dim lights flickering occasionally. Feeling restless, she considered going somewhere to eat, but found herself walking to the town house at a brisk pace instead. When she reached the address and saw Matt sitting on the top step, waiting for her, she didn't feel an ounce of surprise. Instead, she felt instantly calm. The edginess she'd had since leaving Queens subsided, like white noise being cut off.

It was strange, really. In the back of her head, she'd known he would be there. She didn't have time to question why, though, because the intensity in his eyes drew her up the stairs. He stood slowly and she walked right into his open arms. How could it feel so right? She wanted to voice the question, but managed to keep it burning in her chest.

"I need you," Matt whispered into her hair.

"Yes," she answered in kind, knowing she was damning herself and unable to muster the will to deny him anything. Not when she needed him, too. She let them inside, glancing up at Matt questioningly when he took her hand. Expecting him to lead her to the bedroom for a replay of what they'd done earlier, she was surprised when he stopped her at the couch. Saying nothing, he lay down on his side and pulled her down next to him, enfolding her in his arms so tightly she couldn't move. Long minutes passed as she waited for him to kiss her neck or touch her body. His deep, even breaths, however, told her he'd fallen asleep.

Heart in her throat, Lucy tucked her head under his chin and let exhaustion overtake her.

Chapter Sixteen

Matt woke from the deepest sleep in his memory when Lucy rose from the couch. He could tell from the way she tiptoed her way to the kitchen that she thought he wouldn't notice her absence. Or miss her in his arms so much he had to fight the urge to go after her, bring her back to the couch so he could hold her some more. No, he couldn't do that just yet. If he touched her now, she'd end up beneath him with her legs wrapped around his neck. This time, they were going to talk first if it killed him. And thanks to the hard-on he'd woken up with, it just might.

From the darkness of the living room, he watched her through the doorway that led to the lit-up kitchen, as she rummaged through the cupboards for something to eat. Lips pursed, one foot rubbed against the calf muscle of her opposite leg. Her curls were tangled around her neck from sleep. Curls he knew from experience smelled like watermelon. More than anything at that moment, he wanted to lose his hands in her hair, tilt her head back so he could run his lips up her neck. Jesus, his thoughts were doing nothing to ease the tension in his pants. Neither did watching the smooth lines of her throat work as she drained a glass of milk.

When she set the glass down, he could finally see her face. Every licentious thought in his head evaporated at the desolation behind her green eyes. The same one he'd put into them back at the parking garage. Matt rose from the couch and went to join her in the kitchen. She watched him approach warily, giving him a sharp pain in his stomach. He needed a minute to get his head together, so he opened the refrigerator and reached for the first thing he saw. A bowl of grapes. Talking, having an honest conversation, had never been his thing. Listening to people and reading them through their tone was his comfort zone.

He needed to try now. When the explosion on the second floor had propelled him back against the marble wall, when he wasn't sure he'd make it out of the building with the rest of the officers, he'd thought of her. When he'd gone the opposite direction from his team, heading to the bank to finish his assignment of bringing down the target and giving the hostages their freedom, he'd thought of her. Oddly, he'd thought of her playing the accordion. Her husky singing voice, the way her cheeks had been stained pink the entire time. How she'd lifted her chin and kept playing. He'd failed that girl. He'd had his opportunity to tell Brent that he wanted to be with Lucy, permanently, and he'd fucked it up. He'd let his bullshit insecurities get in the way. He could never get that moment back.

If she'd let him, though, he would spend every ounce of energy making it up to her. *If* she still wanted him after she knew about all the ugliness he kept inside. *If* she still thought he was worth it. Worth her. So many ifs, not nearly enough certainties for someone like him who kept everything in its neat little compartment. Lucy couldn't be compartmentalized. That scared the shit out of him even as he craved finally being set free from the grueling requirements he'd set for himself.

Take it slow. Don't scare her. Matt glanced over, commanding himself to say something, anything, to banish the wariness from her face. "Gigawatts."

Her mouth opened and closed. "Huh?"

You are a moronic ass. "I rented *Back to the Future* the other night. It was good." He crossed his arms over his chest. "Completely implausible, but good."

She stared at him. "Why did you rent it?"

Matt almost shrugged off her soft question before remembering his resolve to be honest. No more ignoring things that made him uncomfortable. Not if he wanted a chance with her. "I wanted to be around something you like. I wanted to think of you." Lucy looked dumbfounded. *Too much too soon. Reel it back.* "Changing the past. Fixing mistakes...I wish I could do that sometimes. You know?"

Her expressed grew shuttered. "Mistakes you made with me?"

Matt thought of the way he'd missed his moment in Quincy's to claim Lucy. The rough way he'd taken her the first time. His denying her pleasure in the park. "Yes. With you."

God, he *hated* not being able to read her. She normally had her heart in her eyes at all time, but right now, when he needed her to be an open book, she'd slammed herself shut.

Keep going. "There's a lot more I would fix, though." He paced to the other side of the kitchen, fighting the compulsion to kiss her, distract them both from the conversation.

"Like what?"

Matt searched for the right moment, thankful when Lucy filled the silence he let stretch too long. "When I was fourteen," she said, "my father bought me a dress to wear to my first high school dance. It was horrifying...Day-Glo orange really has no place on a dress." She popped a grape into her mouth, chewed and swallowed. "So I used my allowance to buy a different dress. One that didn't look like bicycle reflective gear. It was such a relief, I thought, but when I walked down the stairs, my father looked so disappointed. Crushed." She lifted one shoulder. "I would go back in time and wear the orange dress. If…gigawatts."

How did she do it? Disarm him so easily while casually eating a grape? He sighed. "Mine is a little worse."

For a moment, she seemed to be wrestling with herself. Then she reached over and flipped the light switch on the wall, casting darkness over the kitchen. "Sometimes it's easier with the lights off."

She was right. Already a little of the weight had eased from his chest. Not all, but some. He needed more, though. Needed to be closer to her. Hoping she wouldn't find it strange, he rounded the table to where she stood leaning against the counter. She stayed perfectly still as he rested his hands on either side of her on the counter and fit their bodies together. Automatically, more of the tightening in his upper body lessened. He laid his cheek against the top of her head, enfolded her in his arms and inhaled deeply.

Lucy.

• • •

She tried, *really* tried, not to relax against Matt. A near impossible feat when he was holding her like he might break otherwise. He still hadn't said anything to clarify his intentions, leaving her with a now-familiar sense of confusion, but the urge to comfort him couldn't be denied. She had the sense that he needed to unburden himself and God help her, she wanted to be the one he did it with. It would ruin her. Instinctively, she knew that. Closed off, Matt was irresistible to her. Once he'd revealed himself, she'd be sunk.

Unfortunately, she'd always been a little reckless. Just never before with her heart. Something told her the consequences would be far worse than being cuffed and stuffed in the back of a police car.

When Matt's fingers skimmed up the back of her neck and cradled her head, she couldn't hold herself back anymore. Her body softened like melted butter against the hard angles of his, eyes closing when he sighed as if relieved.

"Baby."

Lucy's heart squeezed. "Talk to me, Matt."

"You asked me what I would change. If...gigawatts. Funny thing is, I don't even know what I would do to fix what happened." Matt swallowed audibly. "Tommy, my best friend. We joined the service together. Deployed and were stationed together, too." A beat passed. "If he'd been acting differently since we arrived, I just assumed it was because of where we were. The danger involved."

It felt necessary to slip her arms around his waist, so she did. His heartbeat was slightly accelerated against her ear, but somehow reassuring nonetheless.

"It was a roadside bomb. I was driving, he was walking outside the vehicle with three other men. If had been the day before or after, it would have been me. He would have been driving. The randomness of that..."

He cleared his throat. She could feel his hesitation to go on, his guilt and grief. It was palpable in the air around them. "You never know what to expect in that kind of situation, watching your friend die. You couldn't know." A pause. "I didn't expect him to tell me with his last breath that he'd been sleeping with my fiancée."

Lucy pulled back, trying to keep the horror from her face and failing. She didn't know what she'd been expecting him to say. It hadn't been that. "Oh no, Matt."

"He loved her. I could tell. And I realized...I didn't. Not

like he did." His voice took on a faraway quality. "How selfish is that? He must have hated me."

"They were in the wrong. Not you."

Matt looked down at her, then away. "No. I was young and ignorant. I couldn't see what was right in front of me, and I ruined two lives because of it."

"How can you believe that?" she whispered.

He didn't answer her. "I tried to work it out with her, even though I could tell she blamed me for Tommy. Hates me for it. I just thought I owed him, after…"

"God, Matt." His reaction to her initial deception came back in a blinding rush. The anger on his face when he confronted her outside the party. *I don't tolerate liars.* Suddenly everything came into startling focus. *I'm a liar in his eyes. He can't tolerate* me. "You really one-upped my orange dress story," she choked out.

For a moment, she thought the joke had gone too far, but he finally laughed, sounding a little dazed. "Only you, Lucy." His hand coasted over her hair. "That's my past. I'm not going to lie, it messed with my head. I came back to a place I didn't recognize, to people who didn't know me anymore. Everything felt like a lie. Sometimes I still don't feel normal." His rush of breath fanned her hair. "But there's more."

Something about the way Matt's voice dropped caused the atmosphere to shift in the room. He dipped his head and traced his lips across her temple, making her shiver. She wanted to talk more, to tell him none of what happened was his fault. That there were people here, namely his friends, who knew and loved him exactly as he was, but the words felt trapped in her throat. He'd physically and verbally changed the subject, effectively causing her body to take notice.

"More?"

Matt nodded. "Yeah." Using her hair, he tugged her head back, running his tongue up the side of her neck. A decadent buzz raced along Lucy's skin, but it was tempered when she met Matt's gaze. She could feel he was turned on, oh yes, but his eyes were troubled. "I want, I *need*, control, Lucy. Always have. I don't want to scare you away."

Her heart pounded in her chest. She was *terrified* of him, but not in the way he meant. Terrified that she'd given him the power to annihilate her. How'd she get here this fast? It was Matt, he'd pulled her in so deep, so quickly, she hadn't had a fighting chance. Now, curiosity was a living thing inside her. "I don't scare easily," she whispered, already knowing that no matter what he said, she wasn't going anywhere.

He scrutinized her for a beat, then surprised her by reaching for a grape. She watched his teeth sink into its skin with fascination, every muscle beneath her waist clenching at the sight. When he rubbed the remaining half over her lips, coating them with grape juice, heat rushed between her thighs. Needing an anchor, she reached behind her to grip the counter. "Would you like to hear one of my fantasies about you, Lucy?"

She chewed the piece of grape he'd pushed past her lips. "Yes."

Matt began unbuttoning the bodice of her dress, her chest rising and falling beneath it. "You come to my apartment, wearing those jean shorts you had on the day we met. The ones that made my cock so fucking hard, I wanted to bend you over in the coffee shop." When he finally pushed the fabric apart to reveal her breasts, her nipples were hard points. From the drugging quality of his voice, the anticipation of his touch.

He picked up another grape, bit half of it off, then circled her nipples slowly with the remaining half. Somehow the cold sensation sent heat streaking through her center. With a moan, she pushed her breasts higher, begging for more of the same.

Matt popped the rest of the grape into his mouth. Rough hands rose to cup her breasts, massaging them rhythmically. "When you get there, I've made you a meal. Just for you, not me." He bent down to take a deep pull of her right nipple. "I sit you down on my lap while you eat, your bare thighs draped over mine. By the time you finish, you'll be wet because you'll feel me underneath your ass. You'll know what's coming."

Continuing to torture her breasts with long licks of his tongue, his hand slipped up her inner thigh and tugged her panties down, letting them fall to the floor. Lucy felt like her lungs might explode from the racing of her breath. "What happens next?"

Before she could anticipate his next move, he boosted her up onto the counter and spread her legs, baring her damp center. He tested her with one finger, licking his lips slowly, and Lucy swore she heard herself moan. "I push your shorts down to your knees and sink in. You grip the table and ride my dick until your legs give out. Then I put you facedown on the table and finish you off hard."

Yearning twisted in her belly. "Th-that sounds doable."

A corner of Matt's mouth twitched, but his eyes remained mysterious pools. He reached over and picked up another grape, placing it between Lucy's teeth. "Do not bite down. Keep it right there. And close your eyes."

After a moment, she nodded, trusting him to help her fight the insistent ache he'd built. When her eyes slid shut, she felt Matt's tongue drag up the inside of her thigh. Strong hands palmed her bottom, pulling her to the edge of the counter and tilting her at an angle. His mouth nuzzled her core, lips brushing over her sensitive skin. Then he tasted her, humming in his throat, taking his time. Balancing herself with one hand on the counter, Lucy urged him closer with impatient fingers in his hair. She needed relief, couldn't last much longer in this heightened state of arousal. Matt seemed to sense her overwhelming need because his lips closed around her clitoris, worrying it, before sucking it long and deep.

Her teeth sank into the grape with a cry. Already the pressure between her legs was whipping around, looking for an outlet. She could feel half of the grape sliding between her breasts, down her belly, but she didn't care. Matt's tongue was circling her now in tight strokes, big hands massaging her backside in time with his mouth. Her thighs began to shake. *More, more.*

Matt's mouth stopped and he straightened, thumb running over her bottom lip as she gasped for air. "You bit down. Now we have to try again."

"Matt, *please.*"

"Shh." His hand dropped from her mouth to massage the bulge behind his fly. With his other hand, he replaced the ruined grape with a new one in her mouth. "Trust me to make you feel good. Trust me to be obsessed with making you come, Lucy."

Her pulse jackhammered in her ears. Not just from what he'd said, but the way he looked at her. Could this be enough? This irresistible man wanting her simply for her body? Right now, she didn't have a choice. Her body was making decisions for her. "Yes, Matt."

Firm hands spread her thighs wider on the counter as his skilled tongue brought her to the precipice of climax once more. Half her focus went toward finding that desperately needed peak, the other half concentrating on keeping the grape whole between her lips. Not breaking his rule. She found herself sucking on the fruit, mimicking the movements of his mouth, moaning as her tongue skated over the smoothness. Her orgasm rolled over her in a blissful ripple, making her body tremble and cling to him, riding out every ounce of perfection. Still, she wanted more. Needed to feel his skin moving against her own.

She let the grape fall. "Please. I want you inside me, Matt."

His mouth collided with hers in a hot, wet kiss. "I decide when I'm going to fuck you."

Oh, Lord. Renewed heat coursed through her, suffusing every inch of her body. "Fine. As long as it's now."

Amusement leaped into his eyes, but was quickly extinguished by determination and desire. Keeping his focus locked on her, he unhooked his belt and whipped it through the loops of his pants. The *whoosh*ing noise sent her pulse tripping over itself, a whimper falling from her mouth. She tried to relax as he reached behind her, bringing her wrists together and securing them tightly with the pliable strip of leather, but the pulse between her legs had begun beating out of control once more. Being restrained felt foreign, yet handing over her trust completely to Matt felt freeing. The position made her back arch, displaying her stiff nipples, filling her with seductive power. God, she needed to be filled.

As if he'd heard her internal plea, he drew down his zipper and rolled on the condom he'd removed from his pants pocket. In one swift motion, he dragged her off the counter onto his waiting erection. Lucy screamed in her throat at the sudden fullness. Matt bit into her shoulder and groaned, but wouldn't allow her to wrap her legs around his waist, pushing her knees down when she attempted to bring them higher.

With their height difference, her toes barely scraped the floor, Matt's erection the only thing keeping her upright. She screamed at the sensation, her bound hands scrambling behind her for purchase, but they weren't close enough to the counter. He wrapped her hair around his fist to keep her still, and even the sting of pain was welcome. The anchor she desperately needed. It distracted her from the fullness that had become the center of her universe, filling her, supporting her entire weight. Her nerves felt strung as tight as piano wire, body screaming for relief. Words with no meaning fell from her lips, most of them his name.

"Who decides when you need to be fucked, Lucy?"

"You," she sobbed, attempting to plant her toes on the floor and failing. "You decide. *Please*."

"Please, what?" He bit her ear and tugged. "Please prop you up against the counter and pound into you like the madman you've turned me into?"

"Yes. *Yes*."

"When I'm ready." His teeth grazed her bottom lip. "I've been imagining you bound and begging every minute since I met you. Maybe my whole life. And I'm damn well going to enjoy it."

In a move of desperation, she tried to climb his body and wrap her legs around him once more, but he pushed her sweat-slicked knees down. The heavy fall of her legs impaled her on him even further and another scream ripped from her throat. She tugged at her restrained hands and saw Matt's eyes flare, a groan escape him, when she couldn't get free. It ratcheted her need even higher, tightened the growing ache in her belly. The realization that she could orgasm just like this, watching Matt want her, flitted through her buzzing head. She forced herself to still, even though her breaths were coming out sounding more like gasps. Tension built in her belly and she let her head fall back, still being held up by Matt's grip in her hair. She could feel her climax looming like an oncoming storm.

"No, you don't. Not until I allow it." He tugged her head back up with a growl. At the same time, he walked her backward toward the counter. As soon as the hard surface met her lower back, she wrenched her legs high and circled his hips with a cry. She was heedless of anything but chasing relief. The feel of Matt's unyielding body. Again and again, she rolled her hips, her thighs shaking from gripping his body so fiercely.

"Ah fuck, baby, I love it when you work me like that." He pressed his forehead against hers and drove into her *hard*. His gruff moan filled her ear. "Christ. This is why I make you wait. One thrust and you're already clamping down around me. It makes me goddamn crazy."

When he stilled inside her after only that single drive, she cried out. "No. *No.* Please don't stop."

Desperate, mindless, she kissed him without holding anything back. Showing him with her mouth how badly she needed him to move. Requiring oxygen, she finally broke away. "Harder. More. I want all of you. Everything."

Matt's eyes were intense, breathing harsh. "When you kiss me like that, I'll do anything you want." His throat worked. "Maybe I should have kept that secret to myself."

She struggled to focus on his words. "No. I like knowing you have a weakness."

He shook his head. "You have no idea, do you?"

Lucy was growing restless. His body was locked inside hers, thick and throbbing. Her nerve endings snapped everywhere their skin touched. The longer he remained unmoving, the more the ache grew. It was dense and demanding, crying out to be assuaged. On top of it all, possibly more potent than anything, were his eyes. They were coated with lust, but somehow darkly excited by the control he had. In turn, it made her feel powerful. Made her question who was really in control after all. With that thought in mind, she arched her back on the counter and tossed her head back, putting her stomach, her breasts, her throat on display. Tempting him.

Matt growled. "Mine."

"Prove it," Lucy whispered.

Chapter Seventeen

Possessiveness, furious and consuming, laced through Matt's system. She was spread out in front of him like a goddess and he had the honor of being buried inside her. Every second that passed made him hotter, heightening the anticipation of that moment when he would fuck her into the screaming orgasm she deserved. He'd taken her too quickly the first three times and he'd regretted it afterward, wishing he'd taken time to savor her. Even now, his body shook with the need to slide his cock out and ram it back into her slick heat. Knowing she'd love it, would whimper and writhe for more, only made it twice as difficult to deny the urge.

The physical nature of his need was only heightened by the connection he felt to her. Beauty shone out of her and wrapped around his throat. She was the one thing that had been missing his entire life without him realizing it. How had he been walking upright, talking, accomplishing things this long without her?

Savor. He ran his fingertips up the center of her body to tease her nipples. "You asked me what the extent of my need for control is…" Unable to stop himself any longer, he eased his hips back and rolled them forward, memorizing the way her hands clawed at the counter, her lips parted on a moan. "When I walk in the front door after a shift, Lucy, I want your mouth on mine before I even get my jacket off."

Matt let one hand circle her delicate neck lightly as he drove into her again. And again. He couldn't stop now, not with her clenching around him like that. Not with her tasty little nipples pointing straight up as her chest heaved, her body undulated.

"I want to punish you in the mornings, so I can spend the day thinking about your sweet, pink ass, thinking about ways to soothe it when I get home." He reached behind him and grabbed her ankles, raising them above her head. His Lucy liked that. It put him right where she needed him to be, bumping against her luscious clit. He could see the tremors race across her abdomen, feel her feet flexing in his hands. God yeah, she was close.

"Faster, Matt," she gasped. "Please, *please*."

A growl broke from his throat. He'd never get used to her begging for him. Or the fact that she *loved* doing it. Loved submitting to him the way he needed.

"I want to tie your delicious little body up and fuck you. For hours. Until the goddamn sun comes up." He rolled his hips inward, then pressed down, rubbing the base of his erection against her sensitive bundle of nerves. "I want to fall asleep with your gorgeous ass cradling my satisfied dick. Your breasts in my hands. I *need* it, baby."

"*Yes.*"

The way she continued to encourage him…warmth expanded in his chest. Made him want more of her. *Damn.* He couldn't go as fast as she needed at this angle. With each drive of his body, she inched back slightly on the slippery surface. With a growl, Matt yanked her off the counter and wedged her against the cabinet, supporting her hips with his forearm so she wouldn't be hurt. The position bent her in half and put her ankles up around his ears. Matt shouted a curse at the ceiling it put him so goddamn deep. Every slick inch of her was like a manacle around his driving cock.

She threw her head back on a sob and began to shake. *Almost there. Come on, pretty baby.* "Oh, Jesus…*Matt*…"

Just a little more, and she'd blow. "Lucy, if I wake you up at two a.m., dying to eat your pussy, I want you to open your thighs and say *yes, please, Matt.* Do you *understand* me?"

"*Yes*, yes…*oh*." He felt the telltale squeeze grip him and pushed hard into it, holding deep so he could feel her quake all around him. It was the closest to heaven he would ever get and he absorbed every shudder, every word. Eyes appearing blind in the dim light, she chanted things that made no sense, still pinned to the counter by his hips. "*Matt*."

After a moment, the tension in her lessened slightly, but not completely. He was still hard enough inside her to break through steel. Seeing his woman rosy and satisfied in front of him shot a fresh surge of hot, pulsing adrenaline through Matt. Her chest rose and fell on gasping breaths when he twisted his hips, to let her know they weren't finished. *Oh no. We're far from done. You're going to get it again.* She must have read his thoughts on his face because her lips parted on a breathy moan and she nodded.

She's perfect for me. I want to be perfect for her. He released one of her legs and let it drop to his side, continuing to hold the other by the ankle. Keeping his eyes trained on her face, he moved it across his body, slowly turning her around so she faced the counter, remaining inside her the entire time. A sweat broke out on Matt's forehead at the twisting sensation, the inside of her body stroking him sideways as she turned. By the time he had her completely shifted around, he'd gone a little insane.

He forced her up against the counter, unable to stop himself from sinking his teeth into her neck. Lucy tilted her head on a cry. "I'm going to fuck my little spinner now. She's had it too easy so far." With a hand on the back of her neck, he urged her facedown onto the cool surface, hands still secured behind her back with his belt. It put her ass on display for him and he had no choice but to slap that tempting flesh, once, twice, before surging into her. Her knees gave out, slamming into the cabinet beneath them as she screamed. "Feel that, Lucy? That's as hard as it fucking gets."

"*More, please. Again.*"

His vision blurred around the edges at her husky request. Never. He'd never had this part of him accepted before, countered so perfectly, and it felt like coming home. He wanted to shout at the rightness of it, but his body was begging to be relieved. Everything before now suddenly felt insignificant. This is where he belonged. *She* was where he belonged.

Matt reached down and gripped her shoulders as he rode her. His hips bucked against her hard, bringing him in and out of her with blissful friction. Their groans mingled with the sound of smacking flesh, sending him toward his peak quicker. With a final drive, he came with a roar, feeling as though his soul were expanding even as his body depleted. He fell on top of her, giving in to the compulsion to hold on to her. In fact, he couldn't hold her tight enough. In his current state, the irrational fear slipped in that she could be taken away from him and he actually bared his teeth over the thought, tightening his grip.

"My Lucy," he whispered fervently into her hair, kissing the fluttering pulse at her neck.

Words he'd had such a hard time coming by in the past swirled around his head now, bumping into one another at breakneck speed. They wanted to pour out of his mouth for

Lucy to hear, but he determinedly kept them in check. He'd said enough for now. Bravely and beautifully, she'd accepted his need for control. Embraced it without question. He couldn't ask her for more now. If she knew what he wanted with her, what he *intended* to have with her, she might get spooked. He needed to take it slow. More importantly, he needed to do this right.

That's why first thing tomorrow, he was going to find his best friend and tell him the truth. He'd fallen in love with Brent's sister and there wasn't a goddamn thing in this world that could keep him from trying to make her love him back. His life, the happiness he'd never hoped for or expected, depended on keeping her. Her keeping *him*.

After kissing her hair one final time, Matt released her hands from the leather belt, cradling her against his chest and carrying her to the back bedroom. He wanted more than anything to lie down beside her and sleep, but he wouldn't allow himself the privilege yet. Not until he'd done the honorable thing, thereby giving legitimacy to their relationship, even if *relationship* was a puny word to describe what they had.

They were connected.

Eyes closed, she snuggled into the pillow, already appearing half-asleep. Jesus, he could have stood there all night looking at her, reveling in the fact that he'd exhausted her energy.

"Matt?"

Lucy calling his name from bed, all rumpled curls and flushed cheeks. He tucked the memory of it away for later and leaned down to kiss her forehead.

"I'm going to go now, baby."

"You are?" She sat up, holding the comforter over her breasts. "Oh...I'll let you out."

"Stay here. Sleep." Matt tugged the bedding back down and tried to communicate with his eyes what he wouldn't allow himself to say out loud yet. When he finally slept with her in his arms, there wouldn't be a hint of doubt or wrongness lying between them. "We can't keep sneaking around like this. I need to do the right thing, Lucy."

With a nod, she started to lie back down, then changed her mind and leaned up to kiss him. It wasn't a see-you-later kiss. No, she obviously had something else in mind. She appealed to his dominant nature by letting her head fall back on her shoulders, so that he towered above her where she lay vulnerable in the bed. Her mouth parted on a sigh, tongue sliding into his mouth like an offering. Matt nearly lost his balance, her taste, her surrender had such influence over him. A split second before it became impossible for him to do anything but follow her down into the pillows and never leave, she eased back.

Matt took a final inhale of her scent. "I'll be there tomorrow. At the bench."

"You will?"

If he hadn't gotten so lost in her, he might have spent more time scrutinizing the odd expression on her face, but all his focus went into leaving before he could no longer manage it.

He nodded, commanding himself to stand. "Bye, Lucy."

She watched steadily him from the pillow. "Bye, Chuckles."

Chapter Eighteen

Lucy sat on her grandparents' bench in Central Park and stared across the green expanse of lawn that seemed to stretch for a mile, before disappearing into the trees. Absently, her fingers traced the carving of the familiar names inside a heart, just to the right of her thigh.

Virginia and Frankie Mason Until the World Stops Spinning.

Knowing five minutes from now would be the sixtieth anniversary of her grandfather's proposal to her grandmother, she tried to muster a smile, but it withered and died on her face. Instead of commemorating the event, she felt like she was tainting it with her nervous energy. She took a deep breath and closed her eyes, trying to picture her grandmother in a fashionable hat, ankles crossed primly and sitting in that very spot. The man she'd been crazy about for months sat beside her with sweaty palms, an engagement ring burning a hole in his pocket. Lucy remembered the proposal story by heart and replayed it now, hoping it would serve to distract her from the uncertainty threatening to topple her over.

Frankie Mason rolled the newspaper in his hands and

tapped it on his knee.

So I was thinking, Virginia…

Yes, Frankie. I'll marry you.

Aw, swell.

The beginnings of a smile played around Lucy's mouth, but it vanished when Matt took her grandfather's place in her memory and she replaced Virginia. Instead of Frankie Mason's gentle face, Matt's gray eyes watched her steadily from across the bench, a wealth of mystery behind them. She wanted so badly for him to come closer, to hold her as tightly as he had the night before in the kitchen, but instead he got up and walked away. Lucy shook her head to dispel the image, but it stubbornly remained. Unlike him last night, it might never leave her.

She thought back to the afternoon in the coffee shop. With her master's degree under her arm, she'd thought herself invincible in every aspect of her life. Then Matt had walked in and blown that theory right to hell. Perhaps she'd been naive. She hadn't been prepared to feel so much for him, to want him to this stunning degree. Holding herself back around him hadn't been an option and now she sat on this bench, feeling stripped bare. As if parts of her were walking around outside her body and she had no way to get them back.

Last night, she'd been so sure he felt something more. He'd talked about them in the future tense, he'd held her against him so damn tightly, as if trying to fuse them together. Yet he'd gotten out of there so fast, the town house might as well have been on fire. Had she misread him? She couldn't get past the relentless worry that their relationship had begun and ended with her lie that very first afternoon. Perhaps he'd never gotten past it, and any other outcome had been wishful thinking on her part. In fairness, she hadn't been with a lot of men. And certainly none like Matt. The kind of man who could tie you up in knots, then yank them tighter and tighter until you imploded. The kind of man who gave your body and mind an equal workout. After he'd opened up to her last night, she'd thought they'd reached some kind of turning point. He wanted her to understand what made him who he is. What he didn't realize? She'd embraced that man on day one. Back in the motel room, she'd *seen* him. She'd *known* him. As much as he allowed someone to know him.

Two years ago, she'd left behind the daredevil and focused on being the Lucy her family needed. How had she missed the fact that Matt was the equivalent of skydiving without a parachute? Instead of listening to his signals, recognizing that he didn't want anything from her beyond a physical arrangement, she'd let him get close, shown him a part of herself she'd never known existed. Her confidence had built with every encounter. Then he'd stolen it, taking all her progress along with it.

Still, *still*, there was a stubborn voice in her head telling her she'd read Matt right. He cared about her. He was not a fickle man, nor was he the type to play games with someone's emotions. Which is why she sat on her grandparents' bench, praying like hell he showed up. He'd made it to every single event on her itinerary thus far. If he managed to show up this morning, to the only important item on her list, she would fight for them. She would tell him she'd fallen for him and he better get used to having her around. She would shout and curse and stomp until he figured out she was worth it. That *he* was worth it.

If he showed up.

Almost afraid to look, Lucy glanced down at her watch. One minute. He had one minute to get here before she went with option B.

Paris.

She hadn't based the decision solely on Matt, although claiming he had nothing to do with her moving to France would be a lie. Being in the same city with him, knowing she could run into him at any time and relapse into how she felt right now, would be counterproductive to getting over him. And getting over him would be her only option. Being a glorified booty call did not work for her, particularly when it meant going behind her brother's back. No, she couldn't do it. Frankly, she was surprised Matt *could*. Another way she'd misjudged him?

Lucy felt a hint of panic creep into her stomach as the minute came and went, took a deep breath to calm her racing pulse. Conversely, her heart dulled in her chest, feeling heavy. France would not just be an opportunity to put this life-changing week with Matt in her rearview, it would be her chance to help provide for her family. To shift the load from Brent's shoulders onto her own. To keep her parents comfortably retired in Florida. With the new baby coming, her brother would need all the help he could get, even if he would never say it out loud.

She thought of the phone call she'd received last night. They had offered her the job at the Met, right here in New York City. She could take it and stay. It would be a healthy enough salary to give her a start on her own *and* pitch in with her family. But at that moment, it occurred to her that this wasn't her home any more. Hadn't been in a long time. Friends had moved on, her family had flourished in her absence. She'd been here less than a week and she'd managed to jeopardize the friendship between Matt and her brother *and* convince Hayden to lie to Brent. Her leaving town could very well be the best decision for everyone.

What did she have keeping her here? Against her better judgment, she'd let herself consider that Matt might be a reason to stay. She recognized now the fantasy world she'd been living in. They'd been an extended fling, plain and simple. His expressive gray eyes appeared in her head, but she pushed them aside, even if the finality of the action caused her heart to wrench painfully.

Lucy glanced one more time at her watch, shocked at how much time had passed. Thirty minutes late. Could one be late if they never planned on coming in the first place?

She pulled her cell phone out of her purse and sent an email to her contact at the Louvre.

• • •

Matt threw his car in park at the curb and jumped out, Lucy's itinerary still clutched in his hand. Late. He was late. Only by forty-five minutes, but he couldn't shake the horrible feeling of dread pooling in his stomach. Had she waited for him?

He'd been called in early this morning, by the commissioner himself, to make a statement about yesterday's explosion. Four goddamn times he'd repeated the same story for different levels of NYPD brass, without changing a single word. Then the paperwork had begun. By the time he'd finished, he'd glanced at the clock to find it was three o'clock.

He'd resolved to tell Brent this morning about his feelings for Lucy. Hell, he'd been eager to come clean. This afternoon was going to be his chance to claim her. To hold her, no barriers between them. Now he'd missed the most important part of her visit to New York. An event sixty years in the making and he'd fucking missed it. He couldn't help but feel like he'd also missed his deadline to legitimize his relationship with Lucy.

Feeling sick at the thought, he picked up his pace, skirting past people strolling along the path. She would wait for him. Wouldn't she? As much as he'd tried to resist her, this week had been the best of his life. When he was around her, some of her lightness seeped into him. But he needed her *with* him to feel it. It didn't work when she wasn't there.

The bench came into view and he slowed to a stop on the path. Empty. On the spot, he felt that same emptiness invade him. She'd left. She hadn't waited. For a moment, he allowed himself to hope he'd made a mistake and this was the wrong bench, but as he drew closer, he saw the carved words and his hope evaporated.

It was possible she'd never come at all. He thought back to the odd expression on her face the night before when he told her he'd be at the bench this afternoon. The way she'd kissed him with such finality, as if saying good-bye.

Maybe after the way he'd revealed himself last night, telling her in explicit terms the power he wanted in their relationship, she'd made her choice. The right choice. The choice to live in the sunshine without him. He couldn't blame her, even as his heart felt like it was splintering into a million tiny pieces. She would be happier this way. When it came to her, he didn't get to be selfish. It didn't matter that his brain chanted *mine, mine, mine* and urged him to turn the hell around and go find her, convince her to be his. He cared about her too much to do that. She deserved to be happy. And after last night, she must have realized happiness wouldn't be possible with him. She might have temporarily enjoyed what they'd done physically, but in the end it had proven too much, just as he'd predicted.

Matt fell back onto the bench and traced the carving with his fingertips, mentally willing Lucy to sit down beside him. She wouldn't. He knew that. But it didn't stop him from picturing a different outcome. Her crawling onto his lap, telling him the story of her grandparents' proposal. Her eyes sparkling up at him, fingers toying with the buttons of his shirt.

Pain hit him hard. Oh God, how was he supposed to function without her? Before Lucy, before he'd known the effect of her presence, his daily routine hadn't seemed so bad. Now, the very idea of going through those same motions seemed pointless. Since meeting her, getting out of bed in the morning had stopped being a chore and started feeling vital. He'd had Lucy to take care of. Better, he'd had the privilege of seeing her, talking to her.

He hadn't gone back to square one.

No, he'd sunk down further than that.

She doesn't want me.

Muscles suddenly aching, Matt rose from the bench and walked away from the last physical reminder he had of Lucy, knowing no amount of time or distance would erase the memories.

• • •

Matt sat on the locker room bench staring at nothing. The last day had been even worse than he'd expected. He could feel every single thud of his heart, suffering along with him in his chest. Breathing continued to be an effort. *In. Out. In. Out.* He couldn't remember driving to the station this morning or walking into the locker room minutes ago. His body had taken over out of self-preservation because it hurt to think.

When he heard Brent and Daniel enter the row of lockers, he didn't even look up. He didn't want to see them or talk to them. Didn't want to hear about their happiness. And for the love of everything holy, he did not want to hear about their wedding plans. Under normal circumstances, he found that kind of talk insufferable. Today, it might send him over the edge.

Yeah right, as if you haven't already gone sailing over the edge.

They both greeted him with grunts, which he returned without meeting their eyes. Matt suspected he'd never be able to look at Brent again without thinking of Lucy. *Oh, God.* Simply thinking her name felt like a spike being driven into his sternum. Trying to distract himself, he stood and opened his locker. Thankfully, his friends were relatively quiet for once, allowing him to dress for his shift without their usual ribbing of one another.

Behind him, Brent flung open his locker door, letting it slam against the one beside it. Matt frowned, finally glancing at a perplexed-looking Daniel.

"Need a hug, man?" Daniel joked.

"I'm not in the mood today, pretty boy."

Daniel didn't press, but Brent thundered on as if he had. "Sometimes I wonder if women were just put on this earth to make men feel like assholes. Who's with me?"

Daniel lifted an eyebrow. "You're asking the wrong guy. Women are kind of my thing." A slow smile spread across his face. "At least, they used to be."

"Yeah, well, maybe you could have talked some sense into my sister." Brent tossed his giant-sized sneaker into the back of his locker with a *bang*. "I certainly couldn't."

Matt went very still. "What happened? Is she okay?"

Brent shrugged jerkily. "She was physically fine when I dropped her off at the airport an hour ago. Mentally, it's anyone's guess."

"Airport?" Matt choked out, fighting a wave of dizziness.

Brent slumped onto the bench, his irritation seeming to drain out of him. "I don't get it. I've barely spent two seconds with the girl since she finished grad school, then she's off to Paris." He rubbed his forehead, oblivious to the fact that Matt's knees were nearly buckling in front of him. "Fuck. Did I give her the impression that I don't want to hang out with her?" His eyes closed on a frustrated sigh. "She called herself a nuisance."

Matt had been holding his badge. Now, it clattered on the ground. He fought the urge to grab Brent and shake him. "*Nuisance*," he enunciated. "She used that exact word?"

The day of the water balloon fight came back to him then in a tornado of words and color. *If I ever hear of you calling yourself that again, I will find you wherever you are and make you sorry. That's a promise.*

Looking miserable, Brent nodded. "She said the position at the Louvre opened early...that it wouldn't wait. I could tell she was lying. I know her. Something was up."

Matt could hardly think over the furious pounding in his chest. Was this her way of sending him a message? If so, she'd taken a serious risk of him not getting it. Like Brent, he didn't buy the story about the position opening early.

He sprang into motion, shoving his feet into shoes and slamming his locker door shut. Unable to think of anything but the consequences of not getting to Lucy before she boarded the plane, he gripped Brent by the shoulders. "Flight number. Terminal. Give them to me, now."

"Why?" Brent's brow puckered, but his friend knew him well enough that it only took a quick study of Matt's face to determine exactly why he wanted to find his sister. "Oh Jesus, Matty. Are you fucking kidding me?"

"No. I need her." He worked to steady his voice. "She belongs with me and I'm going to get her, with or without your help."

"I can't believe you're making me kick your ass two days after you saved my life." He threw up his hands. "Has to be done. It's a rule."

"Set in stone," Daniel murmured, watching them closely.

Matt's patience was rapidly deteriorating. "Look, you can *try* and kick my ass later. I'll give you the first swing. But right now—"

Brent laughed incredulously. "You don't get to schedule your own ass-kicking."

That did it. Whatever composure he'd been able to maintain evaporated. He shoved Brent up against the lockers and held him there. His friend looked too stunned to react, so he pressed his advantage. "Listen to me. I love your sister.

I love her so much I can't wait for tomorrow. To see what she says, what she wears, which laugh she'll use. She's not your sister to me. She's *Lucy*. She's the girl who makes me feel human." Once the words started, he couldn't seem to stop. "I know I'm not who you'd pick for her, I'm probably not even who *she* would pick, but I'll change that. I'll give her everything. Just tell me where she is."

For a moment, the two friends squared off, taking each other's measure. Then slowly, wordlessly, Brent braced a hand on his shoulder. "*If* you were to get there in time, you'd have some serious convincing to do, man. She already accepted the job. You better be up for it."

Convincing? After everything he'd said…done? Panic rolled through him, blood rushing in his ears. He'd let his insecurities rule him, positive she'd run because she didn't like what he'd shown her. Had he been wrong?

A sickening feeling opened up in his stomach as he recalled every word he'd spoken in the darkness their last night together. *We can't keep sneaking around like this. I need to do the right thing.* He'd still been holding back, not giving her a hint as to what he felt, beyond wanting her in his bed. He'd opened up his past as a way to give her his trust, ask for hers in return. She'd likely seen it as an excuse he'd been giving as to why he *can't* trust. He'd only confirmed it for her by neglecting to show up at the bench on time yesterday.

She'd thought *he'd* ended it with *her.*

Oh God, he'd made a massive mistake. She was getting ready to board a plane, thinking he wanted nothing more than casual sex from her?

No. *No.* This couldn't be happening. Matt barely registered moving toward the locker room door when Brent laid a hand on his arm. He turned and met his friend's grave eyes. "JetBlue terminal. I'll text you the flight number. Go get my sister and bring her home."

Chapter Nineteen

Lucy stood at the ticket counter waiting for her boarding pass, every click of the computer keyboard feeling like a nail driving into her skull. It had taken every ounce of her energy to convince her brother that leaving for France so soon was necessary. That the job wouldn't be there unless she jumped on it immediately. In truth, she would have had to make the decision in the next few days, anyway. Putting it off would have only increased the likelihood of her running into Matt again and she simply couldn't handle the emotional fallout from that.

"Paris in June." The attendant, a kind-eyed redhead, smiled pleasantly. "I'm sure it's going to be beautiful. Any reason for the last-minute trip?"

She started to give some generic answer about giving herself a graduation gift, but the truth picked that moment to set itself free. "Kind of...yeah. Some dickhead decided to use my heart to make fertilizer. I've only known him for a week, but I can't turn the corner in this city anymore without thinking about him and his stupid, *stupid* gorgeous face.

And the way he looked at me." She blew a breath toward the ceiling. "I guess I just had something in my teeth the whole time and he was embarrassed to tell me."

"Now, I'm sure that's not true. You seem lovely."

"Well, I'm not. I'm a liar and a nuisance. Ask anyone."

The attendant's fingers began to fly across the keyboard at a frantic pace.

Lucy took pity on the poor girl and shut her mouth, glancing casually at the television in the waiting area, which had a twenty-four-hour news station playing. Several people had gathered beneath it, pointing up at the screen and talking to each other. For the hundredth time that day, she saw the footage of the explosion in Lower Manhattan. It had been everywhere she looked, on the cover of every newspaper, playing on every channel. She'd found it extremely difficult to look at, knowing how much worse it could have been. What she could have lost. *Whom* she could have lost. Lucy started to look away from the screen, then did a double take. Matt's picture suddenly took up half the television, underneath the words *Matthew Donovan, ESU Sniper, Saves Hundreds of Law Enforcement Lives, Hostages.*

Her scalp prickled as she reread it. Why hadn't he said anything? She remembered her brother's words then, when he'd returned home yesterday. *Let's just say Matt picked a good time to start speaking up.* She'd been so relieved to hear Matt was unharmed, she'd completely let the cryptic statement slip her mind. After saving the lives of so many people, he'd come to her directly afterward, holding her close as he slept. As if he'd…needed her. Yet he'd never said why, just kept it all bottled up inside.

What else had he kept to himself?

She was distracted when the attendant pressed her boarding pass into her hand. "You'll want to get to the gate quickly. They're already boarding."

Nodding absently, Lucy began weaving through the crowds of travelers, wheeling her suitcase behind her. Thoughts of Matt continued to intrude on her brain. A new voice telling her she'd missed something. Matt wasn't the type of man who showed up with flowers and fed a girl recycled lines. He communicated in his own subtle ways. Ways that were easy to miss when you were so focused on what he *wasn't* saying. What she felt for him wasn't casual in the least. She'd *needed* to hear him say the same thing that night in the kitchen. Had his opening up about his past been Matt's way of telling her he cared?

Or maybe she just wanted an excuse not to do the best thing for everyone and get on the plane to Paris. Yes, that's what she needed to do. She wouldn't stay in New York on the off chance Matt decided to—

"*Lucy!*"

She'd just reached her gate when Matt's shout washed over her. The hand holding her suitcase handle went slack, sending her luggage crashing to the floor, but it took her another ten seconds to turn around and face him. He stood a few yards away, stillness in a sea of chaos, the way he'd been the night of the engagement party. Perspiration dotted his forehead, eyes a little wild as they scanned her head to toe, snagging on the boarding pass she held. As always, his distinct, male beauty made her chest hurt. He looked out of place in such drab surroundings, his gray eyes cutting through everything in their wake to jump-start her heart.

She waited for him to say something, but he just continued to look at her. Anger prickled along her skin. She'd made it this far and now he was holding her up. For what? More silence?

"What are you doing here?"

Pain clouded his features. "I'm sorry you have to ask me that. You should have zero doubt as to why the hell I'm here."

Lucy shook her head. *No*, she was done trying to interpret

vague declarations. Done with trying to read between the lines. She needed words. Something to reassure her that this thing between them existed outside her imagination. She snatched up her suitcase and kept walking. "Try again, Matt," she called over her shoulder.

Doing her best to ignore him, Lucy got into line, readying her boarding pass and identification, even though every fiber of her being was screaming at her not to get on the plane. She could feel Matt's gaze on her as he drew closer. "Don't get on the plane, Lucy. Please."

She looked up at the ceiling to keep the tears in her eyes from falling. "Why?"

"I went to the bench." His voice sounded raw. "I'm sorry I was late, but I *was* there."

Oh, she wanted to believe him, but with so much uncertainty dancing around them, how could she? "How can I know for sure?"

"*Virginia and Frankie Mason Until the World Stops Spinning.*" His gaze pled with hers.

Lucy's heart leaped into her throat. She wanted to go to him, bury her face in his neck and hang on for dear life, but she needed more. Needed to know this thing between them was real. More than just a convenient itinerary with chemistry thrown into the mix. It had always been more on her end, but what about him?

Her turn at the gate was next. The flight attendant glanced warily at Matt, then reached for her boarding pass. Lucy took a bracing breath, starting to hand it over.

"Gigawatts."

"What?" She and the flight attendant said at the same time, her boarding pass frozen in midair.

Matt shifted on his feet. "You asked me that night if I could go back in time and fix one thing, what would it be. I'm changing my answer." He took a step in her direction, then stopped, as if afraid she might bolt. "I'd go back to the last night we were together and tell you that I've fallen in love with you. That I'll never let you go."

Lucy could barely see him through the blur of tears. The horrible pain she'd had in her stomach all morning faded a little more with every word he spoke. She demanded her feet to move, to go to him, but the intensity in his voice kept her rooted in place.

"You haven't seen persistence, Lucy. You have no idea what it looks like until you've seen it on me. I've fought for my life before and I'm doing it again now. Do not doubt that I will be on the flight behind yours. I will haunt that museum until you give me the time of day. I will *live* there."

Lucy's throat felt so tight she could barely speak, so she ripped her boarding pass in half instead. Matt fell back a step, both hands resting on top of his head, relief evident in every line of his body. She couldn't stand there a moment longer without feeling his arms around her. Leaving her suitcase behind, she covered the distance separating them in three steps and threw herself into arms that banded around her without hesitation. Applause erupted around them, passengers who had witnessed the scene, some of them recognizing Matt from the news.

"Holy hell, Matt." Her voice wavered. "Have I mentioned that when you talk, you really make it count?"

One of his hands tunneled through her hair, turning her head so he could kiss her mouth. "I'm sorry. Christ, I'm so sorry."

A shiver passed through her. "I almost got on a plane."

Matt fell back into the nearest seat, taking her with him. "Don't remind me. Ever again, please."

Lucy held him tighter. "I love you, too. Let's just focus on that."

"You love me." His breath shuddered out at her ear. "You love me?"

She nodded into his neck, inhaling his scent like a drug. How had she thought for one second that living without him was an option?

Matt shook her a little. "Baby, sometimes what I'm thinking doesn't translate into words. You're going to have to badger them out of me until I get better at this, okay?"

"I can badger."

He tipped her face up for another slow kiss, then stood, lifting her in his arms. "I love you. I'll never keep that to myself again. That's a promise, Lucy."

She swallowed a fresh wave of happy tears as he walked them toward the exit. "Give me a ride home for old time's sake?"

Matt's laughter rumbled through her, before he turned serious. "This time, *every* time from here on out, we go home together."

Epilogue

Matt sat in the back of the stretch limousine, arm draped over the black leather seat, waiting for the door of his building to open and Lucy to emerge. She'd been asking for weeks what he wanted for his birthday and he knew she'd been frustrated by his vagueness. He didn't like seeing her irritated, but appeased himself with the knowledge that she'd find out soon enough.

Matt's mouth lifted into a smile, as it had been doing more and more frequently lately. Specifically, the last four months. Since Lucy. She'd taken the position they'd offered her at the Met and promptly been promoted when they saw how competent and dedicated she was to the job. His favorite part of the day had become picking her up from work. Watching her practically float down the endless steps, brimming with news about her day. He still felt the urge to pinch himself every time, in disbelief that this girl could be walking toward *him*. Then she would throw her arms around his neck and everything in his world righted itself.

She'd made a pretense of moving into her childhood

home in Queens, but after spending one too many restless nights away from him, he'd gained her agreement to move into his apartment in Tribeca. It had baffled him, at first, that he'd ever been so comfortable in his solitude. Until he realized he'd just been waiting for Lucy. Then it made perfect sense.

Drumming his fingertips impatiently on the armrest, he thought back to their first week living together. She'd still been acting like a guest, refusing to touch or move his things. One morning after she'd left for work, he'd stood in the middle of the space, looked around and realized it had all the character of a morgue. White walls, gray furniture, black… everywhere. Sort of like his life before she'd come into it. At a total loss, he'd called Daniel's girlfriend, Story, and asked for her help. His apartment was now painted bright-ass pink.

He loved it.

Lucy walked out of the building, effectively putting an end to his concentration. She wore a tight blue sweater-dress and knee-high leather boots in deference to the cooler October temperature. Her strawberry-blond curls had grown out, swaying at her shoulders as she searched for him on the sidewalk. When she caught sight of him sitting in the limousine, her gaze narrowed, but he saw the hint of mischief in her expression. Lucy loved surprises, yet another thing he'd learned about her. *Not enough*, Matt thought, as she sauntered forward. He wanted to know every single thing about her. If she gave him what he wanted for his birthday, he'd have all the time in the world to do it.

Matt stepped out of the limousine and held the door open for Lucy. God, she looked beautiful. Color in her cheeks, eyes sparkling. *Please let me have something to do with that.*

"You rented a limo on your own birthday? I'm officially the worst girlfriend ever."

He shrugged. "I can't drive and keep you distracted at

the same time."

The bloom in her cheeks spread, her lips parted. "That sounds promising."

Matt crooked his finger at her and she pushed up on her toes to kiss him softly, but it wasn't enough. He wrapped an arm around her waist and took a deep pull off her mouth, keeping her against him until that sense of rightness slipped into place, as it always did for him when they were together.

There it is. Matt pulled back, holding her hand as she ducked through the door. He followed her in, signaling the driver to go. He hadn't been lying that one of the reasons he'd rented the limo was to keep her distracted. From their destination.

With a flick of his wrist, he closed the panel separating them from the driver. The second reason didn't need an explanation. Every opportunity to touch her, hold her, would be taken. If that made him selfish, so be it. It was his birthday, after all.

As they pulled away from the curb, he opened his arms and Lucy climbed onto his lap. The way her head tucked under his chin with such perfection caused his eyes to close, even as his heart rate kicked up at having her close.

"Where are we going?"

"You think I've kept you in the dark this long to tell you now?"

"Not even a hint?"

"No." Matt cleared his throat. "Lucy?"

He didn't have to say anything else. His girl knew what he needed to hear. "I love you, Matt. So much. Always." She rubbed a hand down his chest. "I still want a hint."

This is why he'd needed to distract her. If she kept talking to him in her husky voice, touching him at every opportunity, he'd screw this up. With a hand on her chin, he tipped her face up for a kiss. It started sweet, but as usual, the taste of her, the weight of her on his lap, made him hard. His body didn't care that they would be arriving at their destination in ten minutes, it wanted to be tucked snugly between her legs. Lucy's ass circled in his lap and they groaned into each other's mouth. All it would take was a few shifts of their clothing and he'd be seated in her tight heat.

No, that's not what today was about. Later. He'd have to wait until later. Even if it killed him. Matt pulled away, but pressed light kisses to her lips until her breathing evened.

"What did you get me for my birthday?"

Her jaw dropped. "You told me not to get you anything."

"Since when do you listen to me?"

She looked up at him from underneath her eyelashes. "I listen to you all the time."

Yes, she certainly did. The reminder made him want to press her back onto the leather seat and reward her for just how well. "*Outside* the bedroom, Lucy."

"You got me there."

Matt waited, frowning at the way her fingers fidgeted with her skirt.

"Don't overreact. I booked us flights to Florida to meet my parents. They're for next month. But they're refundable."

He grabbed her hand to stop the distracting movements, but he didn't say anything. Couldn't with the lump in his throat. She wanted to introduce him to her parents. Apart from what he hoped to gain from her today, that faith in him was the best present she could have given him. He leaned in and kissed her, long and hard, until he found his voice. "Don't cancel them. I want to go."

Her smile made his chest hurt, so he tucked her head back under his chin. They stayed that way, Matt stroking her hair, until they were a few blocks from their destination. Thankfully, Lucy looked too lost in her own thoughts to determine where exactly they were in the city. Just to be on the safe side, he pulled the blindfold out of his pocket. She didn't flinch or question him when he tied it over her eyes. Her trust in him was so absolute, he wanted to crush her against his chest and never let go. *Soon. Later.*

When the driver opened the door, Matt took Lucy's hand and helped her out. He nodded at the man to wait, then led her down the path. A curious smile curled her lips at the end, but the frown between her eyebrows told her she didn't know their location. Finally, they reached the spot he'd been leading her to and removed the blindfold...to reveal her grandparents' bench.

She looked down at it, then back up at him, tears in her eyes. "Matt?"

He kept his eyes locked on her face as her mother and father stepped out from behind the surrounding trees, along with Brent and Hayden. Troy and his girlfriend, Ruby. Story and Daniel were there, too. Every single one of them was smiling, happy about what he was about to do. Not dreading it, not wishing she would have done better. It made his heart swell until he could barely breathe.

Lucy let out a watery laugh and fell back on the bench. Right where he wanted her. She must have thought such a public proposal was hard for him, because when he got down on one knee, she reached out and clasped his face in her hands, rubbing her thumbs along his cheeks. Didn't she know this was the easiest decision he'd ever made in his life?

"Lucy Mason, you brought the color in. You brought me to life when I didn't even realize I'd stopped breathing." He laid his hand over hers on his cheek. "Now I can't get enough air. It's everywhere because of you." When he pulled the ring out of his jacket and popped open the lid, she didn't take her eyes off his face for a second. "Be my air. Let me be yours. Forever. Marry me, Lucy."

"Yes." She knelt down in front of him on the ground, meeting him halfway as always. "Yes, Matt. Of course, yes."

Everyone he'd invited to the proposal cheered around them, including a few bystanders who'd stopped to witness the scene. He held her tight against him, as the group closed in around them.

"Triple wedding. I hope you're ready," Story said on a laugh.

Lucy laid a soft kiss on his lips. "We're ready for anything."

Acknowledgments

To my husband, Patrick, whose association with my crazy ass finally paid off last year. Look, honey, I've amounted to something! And my darling little girl who stands outside my bedroom door as I type in bed, saying, "Mommy, you workin' in there?" It reminds me *why* I'm working. I love you.

To Heather Howland, who can never be thanked enough. Thank you for being invested in my characters and their futures. Oh, and *my* future! I appreciate everything you do.

To Liz Pelletier, thank you for your amazing notes on this book. They encouraged me to add something I *really* loved that enriched the characters and I hope readers will love it, too.

To Cari Quinn, for being an all-around awesome lady and author. You've become a friend and an encouraging presence in my life who constantly boosts me higher when I need it. Thank you!

To Pamela Symes for translating a rather inappropriate ditty into French for me. And Jillian Stein (J-Sizzle), of ReadLoveBlog, for brokering that last-minute assistance (not to mention, being a superfly babe). Thank you!

To Bailey's Babes, I love you guys! Thank for the daily encouragement and your excitement to read Matt's story. Hope you love him as much as I do.

About the Author

NYT and *USA TODAY* bestselling author Tessa Bailey lives in Brooklyn, New York, with her husband and young daughter. When she isn't writing or reading romance, she enjoys a good argument and thirty-minute recipes.

www.tessabailey.com
Join Bailey's Babes!

Enjoy more heat from Entangled...

WET AND RECKLESS
a Private Pleasures novel by Samanthe Beck

Aspiring singer/songwriter Roxy Goodhart's latest mistake is a doozy, involving a lying ex-manager, a dire lack of cash, and a teensy bit of grand larceny. Landing in the long, strong, entirely too tempting arms of the law is no way to keep a low profile. Taking an apartment puts her under orderly West Donovan and in his path every day. Testing his impressive reserve is beyond reckless, but she'd love to test it...all...night...long.

ONE NIGHT STAND AFTER ANOTHER
a novel by Amanda Usen

Clara Duke lives to crochet wearable art. But right this second, she's looking at the one guy who has the uncanny ability to unravel her in every possible way. *Zane Brampton.* A whole night with this delectable, gorgeous man would be nothing less than a total sexpocalypse. But then Zane wants his chance to prove he deserves more than one night...and he might just be the thread that snaps all of Clara's perfectly crocheted plans.

Printed in Great Britain
by Amazon

31412268R00119